BRIGHT LIGHT

MONIQUE JACOB

Soft cover Edition

Published by Filidh Publishing

Victoria, British Columbia, Canada

ISBN 978-1-927848-15-9

filidhbooks.com

Cover art by Stephen Landry
Cover design by Danny Weeds
Author photo by Geoectomy Photography

Acknowledgements:

I'm happy when beta readers like an early draft of a story. I'm even happier when they find the plot holes, grammar and spelling mistakes, continuity errors and clichés that I so blithely toss in as I make stuff up.

Many thanks to Thomas Keesman, Sarah Johnson, Jennifer Peddle, Peninah Rost, Zoe Duff, Diane Cliffe and Timothy Hellum. Your insight and patience are much appreciated.

And to all the good dogs I've met at the park and on the internet that inspired the creation of Lulu: may you have all the cookies and walks you could ever want.

Other novels by Monique Jacob:

Tye Dye Voodoo

Voodoo Mystery Tour

Short stories by Monique Jacob in:

The UnValentine Anthology

Anthology for a Green Planet

This is for Jack,

who loved to run.

Ambush

Riley Mason peered around the giant oak that stood sentinel where the paths intersected. The massive trunk seemed a lot wider when he was a kid. Now he had to stand sideways to get full cover. He pulled Lulu close. She whined and nosed his hand.

If they could get through the park to the road, the rest of the way would be clear. Mostly. He glanced across the path at the lamp post and its shattered globe. No one would be around to replace the bulb until the city truck showed up on Monday. The moon had barely risen and dark shadows filled every corner of the park. They could be hiding anywhere.

Lulu growled and Riley touched the dog's trembling head. She pushed at his leg insistently, urging him to move. Riley wanted to race across the park like they used to but Lulu was limping worse than ever and he'd been slowing his pace lately so she could keep up.

Riley wished his dog had stayed home today, like she'd been told to, but Lulu had met him after school every day since first grade and today was no different for her. She was old – nearly twelve – and his dad said that made her older than his grandfather, who used a walker to get around and spilled food everywhere when he ate because his hands shook so much.

A breeze swept through the park, rustling a few dead leaves that still clung to mostly bare branches. Riley shivered and zipped his jacket to his chin. Lulu would slow down even more if she got too cold.

He knew those guys were waiting for him, probably hiding behind the thick laurel bushes that bordered the path home. He felt stupid for allowing them to threaten him into stealing another history test. The first time had been bad enough and he'd lost his appetite when his dad bragged at the dinner table about how every single student had passed his latest quiz.

Riley should have trusted Lulu's instincts when she tried to push him toward the street to take the long way around the park, but she'd been panting and he'd cut through the park so they'd get home quicker. He understood now that she'd been anxious, not tired. He took a deep breath and touched her head again. She snuffled his fingers and gently nipped them. They had to go.

"Come on, girl," Riley whispered.

He rounded the tree and stepped onto the path. The gravel crunched loudly under his boots and announced his presence to those who already knew he was there. He heard a giggle and almost ducked behind the tree again.

Lulu barked a warning as two boys from Riley's school came out of the shadows to face him. The Trimble twins had been terrorizing Riley since fifth grade. High school hadn't changed anything. They still dressed alike, to the confusion of their teachers and anyone else they wanted to torment. Riley could tell them apart but only if they stood side by side.

Jody and Jerry came in fast, aiming for Lulu who snapped at their fingers and drove them back. She barked and showed her fangs to the two identical round faces. Lulu pressed her body against Riley's legs, trying to push him toward the road.

"You should have left Fifi home." This voice came from the left. Riley turned to face Matt White standing shoulder to shoulder with Adam Shea, Riley's best friend.

Scratch that, Riley thought. Ex-best friend.

"Her name's Lulu," Adam said, breathlessly.

"Don't care what the mutt's name is, dumbass," Matt said, circling to avoid Lulu. "I'm just saying Fifi can't protect him from four of us." He skipped back when she snapped at his fingers.

"What are you doing with these losers, Adam?" Riley could just make out the fading bruise around Adam's left eye, where Matt had punched him two weeks ago. Riley had escaped that particular beating by running out into traffic. He'd ignored angry drivers blasting their horns as he zipped around cars to the woods on the other side of the road.

"At least they don't leave a guy behind when he's down," Adam wheezed. He dug his inhaler out of an inside pocket.

"They're the ones who knocked you down," Riley cried in exasperation. "You're not making sense."

Adam sucked in a noisy puff of his medicine and held it in his lungs for a moment before turning away to pant and cough. "I know which side," he said, gasping, "to bet on."

"You're betting on the team that was going to beat me even after I'd agreed to steal another test. Do you really think they're your friends?" Riley stared hard at Adam, who dropped his gaze to the ground.

Matt wrapped an arm around Adam's shoulders and squeezed. "We're not just friends, we're family. Right, cousin?"

Adam nodded and kept his eyes down. He heard the twins circling the group and flinched when Jerry tapped his cheek. "Enough chit chat, girls."

"You should've just left the answers blank again." Jody punched Riley in the face and grinned when bright blood spurted from his nose. "If I flunk History, you'll get way worse than this." He flexed his hand and shook it out.

"Hold him."

Riley tried to lunge away but his head was spinning from the punch and he only managed to stagger into Jerry, who pulled Riley's hands away from his face and wrenched them behind his back.

The Trimbles were a year older than the rest of them, heavier and stronger. Riley's broken nose shifted painfully as he flinched at Jody's feinted left. His eyes flooded with tears of pain but he still caught Jody's gleeful expression as the bigger boy flew in with both fists, punching up into Riley's ribs. All the air was forced out of his lungs as his chest took the punishing blows. Jerry let go of his arms and Riley folded to the ground.

Lulu was barking shrilly and trying to bite the twins' legs but only managing to nip at their jeans while she barely avoided the kicks they aimed at her. She stumbled and fell heavily, yelping as she landed on her sore hip.

Adam moved to help Lulu but Matt yanked him back by his jacket and sneered in his face. "I knew you'd turn out to be a pussy." He shoved Adam away in disgust. "I'll take her out myself."

Matt circled to get behind Lulu. Adam followed closely. He didn't want the beating that Riley was getting so was sticking close to his cousin, who had promised he wouldn't hit him. The twins had made no such promise.

Lulu climbed awkwardly to her feet. She jabbed Adam with her snout, pushing him toward Riley. Her body language was clear: let's go!

Adam had known her since she was a puppy. He had played with Lulu and Riley on the lawn between their houses until they were old enough to cross the main road and explore the woods. He reached for her but she barked sharply and turned back to Riley.

Matt blocked her way. Lulu tried to go around him but she was limping heavily from the fall and he was too quick. "Where you going, Fifi?" Matt swung his foot back and, with a whooping yell, kicked Lulu hard under the chin. Her head snapped up and her body followed in a graceless somersault. She landed on her side, her nose bleeding and her jaw askew.

Riley hadn't yet managed a full breath but felt like he'd been punched in the gut a second time when Matt's boot connected with Lulu's chin. He willed her to move, feeling sick at the sight of her still form.

Matt slapped Adam on the back of the head. "Come on, cousin. He screwed you over too." He pushed him toward Riley, who was trying to crawl to Lulu with one arm wrapped around the flaming pain in his ribs. Jody and Jerry walked alongside him and took turns knocking him flat with a kick or a shove. They yanked on his backpack, trying to dislodge it, but it was secured by a waist strap that jerked upward into his ribs with every tug.

Riley shook with pain and fear but was determined to reach Lulu. He hoped she was breathing but couldn't take his eyes off the spreading pool of blood that glistened black in the moonlight.

"Come on, Adam," one of the twins taunted as he jabbed Riley again between the shoulder blades. "Don't you want to join in the fun?"

Riley shivered at Jody's chilling tone as he struggled up once more. He'd always been more afraid of the twins than of Matt since the day he'd seen them chop off the tail of one of the neighborhood's stray cats. They'd laughed the whole time, imitating the cat's yowls of pain, which amused them even more. They were now eying Adam the same way they'd looked at that cat.

Riley dug his elbow into the grass to drag himself forward but someone stepped between him and Lulu. "Haven't you guys had enough fun for one night?" he mumbled through a mouthful of blood. Riley recognized Adam's boots planted in front of him and for a second thought he was there to help him.

The twins took positions on either side of Adam, hemming him in place. Riley could only see tiny slivers of Lulu between the three pairs of legs. She still hadn't moved and it was too dark now to see if her chest was rising.

"We're not finished with you yet." The voice was behind him but Riley couldn't turn around to face Matt; he couldn't take his eyes off his dog. Every part of his body hurt and all he wanted to do was lie down in the cold grass, but he had to find out how badly Lulu was hurt.

"Adam's going to show you what happens when you betray your friends," Matt continued, prodding Riley's ribs with the toe of his boot. He grinned at his grunt of pain and gestured to Adam. He hoped his cousin realized he was in danger of failing more than a history test. If Adam bailed now, the twins would give him worse than what they gave to Riley.

Jody and Jerry jostled Adam, screeching laughter in his ears like a pair of hyenas. They both had terrible breath, as if they'd never brushed their teeth their whole lives.

"Riley, I'm…" Adam started. He stumbled and stepped on Lulu's paw. She made no sound. "You should have told me the answers were fakes," he continued lamely.

"We studied together. You could have passed it." Riley spat blood onto the dry winter grass. "I didn't think you'd be stupid enough to cheat."

 "Quit stalling," Jody hissed in Adam's ear. "It's do or die." Adam gasped in pain as his arm was twisted behind his back. He glanced sideways at Jerry, who winked at him and made a show of cracking his knuckles.

Riley didn't see Adam raise his foot, but felt the boot heel slam down onto his left hand. He heard the crunch of many bones breaking and cried out as his arm stopped supporting him and he collapsed onto his face. He lay on the grass, barely able to breathe as the twins whooped and laughed.

His hand felt like it was full of glass shards. It was excruciating and it momentarily dimmed the pain in his ribs and face. He'd learned how shock can numb pain and welcomed that numbness as he pulled himself with his good arm toward Lulu. Adam wasn't in his way anymore but was bent over a bush, retching and crying.

Riley whimpered in fear at Lulu's crushed face. Jagged, broken teeth lay in the grass near her smashed jaw. He had a sudden flashback of when he was six and had lost one of his front teeth. It was sitting on his palm for his parents to admire when Lulu slurped it up and swallowed it. He'd tried to punish her by ignoring her for the rest of that day but his dad convinced him that she had no idea what she'd done wrong and he helped Riley write a letter to the tooth fairy, explaining what had happened so he'd still get his quarter.

He couldn't tell if Lulu was breathing and was reaching with his good hand to touch her when, suddenly, the entire park lit up. He turned his head and squinted at the others in the blinding light. Their mouths were open and they were spinning around trying to see where it was coming from.

Every shadowy space in the park was exposed in the white glare. The air was filled with a loud, throbbing hum and dry leaves whipped around them in the rising wind.

"Run for it," Matt yelled. "It's the cops!"

Jody and Jerry laughed wildly as they ran, and Riley saw Adam pause for just a moment before following the others. He'd seen a terrible fear in Adam's face, tinged with regret.

Riley didn't care. He collapsed next to Lulu on the grass. He nudged her and got no response. Her chest was still. Lulu's blood speckled the dried grass near his face. The deep red stood out against the yellowed ground cover and Riley stared at it as the brightness intensified until everything was searing light and crushing noise, assaulting and overwhelming his senses so that he wasn't even aware when the noisy light became quiet dark and he passed out.

Adam Stomp

Riley opened his eyes and blinked in the near darkness. He was lying on his side and could feel dampness seeping through his jacket and jeans from the wet ground. As his eyes adjusted, vague gloomy shapes became trees, rocks and bushes. He could just make out a gravel path.

He was in the park. He laid perfectly still, listening for Matt and the others, but heard only traffic in the distance and wind blowing through the branches overhead. They were gone. He sighed in relief, moving carefully so he wouldn't aggravate his injuries.

Lulu whined and poked her cold nose in his ear. Lulu was whining? Riley's heart raced. They'd been savagely beaten. His dog should be unconscious and bleeding, not whining.

Riley sat up gingerly, hunched to protect his bashed ribs. But the searing agony he'd anticipated wasn't there. He probed the sides of his ribcage but there was no pain, even when he pressed hard. He let out the breath he hadn't known he was holding.

He'd been dreaming. He'd fallen asleep waiting for those guys to leave, and dreamed that he and Lulu had been beaten up. It felt so real, so vivid, like the worst nightmare he'd ever had. His dad always said that his mind would make a mess of reality, if he let it.

Riley got to his feet while Lulu chuffed and prodded him, clearly anxious and wanting his full attention. No beating, so no injuries, though his left hand ached dully. He'd probably slept on it. He shook his hand and winced at a sharp twinge.

"What the hell?" The tip of his pinky angled outward and the next two fingers didn't quite straighten out all the way, curving down like claws. He waggled the fingers. They moved stiffly and he couldn't completely close his hand.

Lulu growled. She sniffed the air and trotted to the gravel path.

Adam stomp.

He heard the words clearly though they weren't spoken aloud. Riley stared at his dog, wondering if he was still dreaming. He'd always talked to Lulu, making up her end of the conversation, but those words had just popped into his head as if Lulu had really said them.

 "Right," he said slowly. "I knew that. Adam stomped on my hand with his boot heel." He flexed his fingers again and felt an aching tension as he tried to make a fist. "I felt the bones break." He shook his head to clear it and blinked hard, but the fingers didn't change. Still crooked.

Adam stomp Riley.

"You *are* in my head!"

As weird as that was, he couldn't shake an eerie feeling that it was normal, like his busted hand that was magically healed. He was still wearing his backpack and jacket but they felt uncomfortably tight. He called Lulu to him and his eyes widened in surprise. "Whoa, what happened to your teeth?" Riley grabbed a handful of the long silky fur under her chin to keep her head still. Lulu wriggled and growled while Riley lifted the sides of her lips to check her mouth. Where he'd expected to find broken teeth and lots of blood there was only smooth white enamel with no gaps, and no fangs. Lulu wrenched her head away.

 "We were right over there," Riley murmured. He searched the ground until he found what he had hoped he wouldn't – a flattened section of grass matted with tacky blood. Several tiny objects clung to the bloody grass. Lulu's teeth, cracked and jagged where they'd been bashed from her jaw. Riley closed his fist around them and the sharp edges pressed into his palm.

Go now.

Riley felt a prickle of unease and peered into the deepest shadows at the edges of the park. Nothing moved but he'd already been fooled once today. Those guys had ambushed him and Lulu. They could be hiding anywhere, waiting to jump them again.

He closed his eyes and took a calming breath. It went all the way in and out easily – no way his ribs were cracked and bruised just a while ago. It had to be a dream, but if it hadn't happened why was Lulu's nearly-fresh blood on the grass? Had they been attacked or was he going crazy?

The blood and broken teeth on the grass were real. His healed but deformed fingers were real. They proved the beatings had happened but were contradictory at the same time.

Lulu raced away, stopping at the far edge of the path to bark impatiently.

"Whoa, Lulu," Riley said incredulously. "You're running?" He'd stopped taking her out for runs with his bicycle almost two years ago. The vet said it was arthritis and would only get worse. But she was zipping back to him at full speed, as if she wasn't a twelve-year-old border collie who could barely climb stairs without his help.

Go now!

He flinched, jarred by this strange new reality where the amazing sight of Lulu running again was nothing compared to hearing her shout in his head.

Maybe he really had been badly beaten and was lying unconscious in a hospital. Maybe this was all some weird coma dream. His hand was mangled but fixed. Lulu was running and he could hear her talking in his head. Was he dreaming or just plain crazy?

Lulu ran around him several times before jabbing him hard in the crotch.

That was real.

"Ow!" he squeaked as he bent over. "What the hell?"

Lulu raced away toward the street. Riley limped after her in a crouch. And now he had to pee. That was going to hurt but it proved that he wasn't dreaming. He always woke up if he had to go. Always. So he must be awake. He'd long outgrown waking up in cold wet sheets, and the slightest pressure from his bladder in the middle of the night had him up and stumbling to the bathroom. If he had to pee there was no way he was asleep.

Lulu pee.

The words were growly – more so than the voice he'd made up for her in his head when he was little – but it was undeniably Lulu saying that she was the one who had to pee. Riley had nearly reached the end of the path before he realized his own bladder wasn't full at all.

Lulu squatted in the grass long enough for him to catch up.

"Why are you in such a hurry?"

Go home. Eat chicken.

"What chicken?"

Lulu smell chicken.

Maybe this was all some crazy hallucination from a concussion. But his head didn't hurt any more than his ribs did. His left hand did hurt a little when he flexed it. It wouldn't close completely into a fist. He tried harder and felt a sharp pull that signaled the hand's limit. He shook it out and jammed both hands in his jacket pockets, confused and scared.

The broken ends of Lulu's teeth were tacky with half-dried blood, their edges sharp against his fingertips. The image of Lulu lying still and broken seemed as real to Riley as the Lulu now trotting just ahead of him, acting as if she hadn't just had her jaw smashed by a steel-toed boot. He transferred the fragments to the front pocket of his jeans so he wouldn't lose them.

He glanced left at the moon that was only now a little higher than when he'd first cut through the park. How could he remember being beaten up barely an hour ago but not have any cuts or bruises? Bones take weeks to heal and he'd *felt* his fingers break when Adam's boot heel came down on his hand.

"Lulu, come here." She stopped but her nose and ears twitched constantly as they monitored the smells and sounds around them. She kept looking at the sky and crouching, as if expecting something to come down on her head. Riley glanced up into the treetops, worried that one of those guys was waiting to jump on them, but he saw only bare branches.

"Are you really my Lulu?"

Riley's Lulu.

Riley studied his dog's face. Her brown eyes were clear, with no trace of the murkiness that had dimmed her vision in the past couple of years. The white fur salting her black muzzle was gone. She was slim and muscular and looked as if she'd stepped right out of their past.

"You're different," he said and stroked her silky ears. Lulu licked his hand.

Riley different.

"I feel the same, except my hand hurts a bit and doesn't work so well."

Adam stomp.

Lulu growled and bared her strange flat teeth. Riley blinked at the sight and felt in his pocket again for her broken fangs. He couldn't decide which were real.

"I know," Riley finally said. "He did it because he was afraid."

Adam bully.

Bully. His best friend had joined up with those guys. Adam thought they wouldn't beat him if he helped them go after Riley. Ever since Matt had moved into the neighbourhood, he'd been after Adam to stop hanging out with Riley. Blood was thicker than water, he kept telling Adam, though being Matt's cousin had never saved Adam from a beating.

Go now.

"Wait, please stop. How come I can hear you in my head?"

Special food.

Lulu raced across the grass to their house. She ran up the stairs to the door, then turned to chuff impatiently at Riley.

"Special food?" Riley stopped at the bottom of the stairs and rubbed his temples. He was seriously confused and his brain felt like it was about to squeeze out through his ears. "That doesn't make any sense. What happened to us?"

Lulu peered up at the sky and lifted her lip in a snarl.

Bright light.

Bright Light

Riley was on his back with no ground beneath him. He was floating, like in a dream or maybe in a swimming pool, except he wasn't asleep and he wasn't wet. He opened his eyes to blinding light and squeezed them shut again immediately, grunting from the blazing headache it triggered. His face felt swollen and he tried to bring a hand up to check but couldn't move his arms.

Not just a floating dream then, but one of those where he thought he was awake but couldn't move, caught in a loop that always brought him back to waking up paralyzed. His heart raced and he tried not to panic.

But if he was in bed and dreaming, why could he feel a breeze ruffling his hair? He forced his eyes open again and squinted as the blinding light and cold wind sent tears streaming over his face. He saw movement to his left and managed to turn his

head a fraction, catching a dizzying view of
treetops falling away at an alarming speed.

He was moving upward, and fast. This brought
him to full awareness, and with that came the pain.
His arms were flung out to the sides and his left
hand was a ball of agony, as if he were crushing
broken glass in his fist. His backpack was still
strapped to his back and dangling underneath him.
The full memory of the past few minutes came
back to him like a fresh punch in the head and he
cried out, looking around wildly.

He'd risen far above the treetops and could see
nothing but that brilliant whiteness. He shivered as
the temperature dropped, though the cold soothed
his many cuts and bruises.

Then something warm splashed onto his cheek. It
rolled into his mouth and he tasted coppery
saltiness. Blood? He squinted up into the searing
light and made out Lulu's familiar silhouette at
least twenty feet above him.

Her nose pointed downward and as he watched,
squinting through his swollen eyes, another drop
of blood dripped off her snout. It hit his face so
fast that he felt like he'd moved up to meet it
instead of it falling down to him. Like one of those
math questions about two trains hurtling toward

each other. He tried to call out to her but just the effort of trying to open his mouth hurt his head so much it felt like he'd been smack in the middle of those two trains when they crashed.

No, not trains. That was a stupid math problem. This was something else. What the hell was happening? He'd been heading home from class. Lulu was waiting at the edge of the school grounds like she always did. Then those guys ambushed him and Lulu in the park and he lost count of how many punches and kicks he took. He remembered crawling toward Lulu's unmoving form.

Then this light blasted them and he passed out.

Maybe he and Lulu got more than just a beating – were they dead? You were supposed to go into the light when you died. That's what he'd seen on one of those paranormal myth-busting shows. But you could choose to go, right? He and Lulu were being pulled into the light – like a tractor beam in a science fiction movie – so it couldn't be that kind of light. Could it?

Another drop of Lulu's blood hit Riley's face. He took a breath to call to her and felt his chest spasm with fresh pain. He coughed and tasted more blood. He couldn't be dead if he hurt this much.

He struggled to think as the light became impossibly brighter, its beam more narrowed and focused. He heard a deep muted bleat that throbbed in his bones. It was coming from above and got louder as he and Lulu approached. He thought he heard voices but couldn't make out any words.

Matt was shouting about the police when he ran off. Someone must have called the cops when they saw those guys beating him and Lulu, and they sent a helicopter. Just like on TV or in the movies. Sent in a SWAT team and the riot police.

Get real, he told himself. No one sends in a SWAT team because a kid and his dog got attacked by some other kids. But where was all the noise and light coming from if not a helicopter?

He probably had brain damage from all those punches and kicks to the head. He'd lost count of how many times Jody and Jerry hit him while he was trying to crawl to Lulu. At least if he was brain damaged, he'd never have to go back to that school. He'd never again have to run or hide from those creeps and they'd never be able to bully him into stealing from his dad again.

But there was also the possibility that he really was dead or dying, that the bright light was a death tunnel pulling him through to the other side.

If he and Lulu were dead, it was good to know that dogs went to heaven too.

Riley closed his eyes and that's when several hands grabbed him and dragged him inside a door he hadn't noticed beyond the light.

Furry hands.

With claws.

Not Dream

Riley was dizzy and steadied himself with a hand on the porch railing. He'd had no memory of anything but the ambush until Lulu said the words. Then it was all there: the brilliant light splashing over everything, the guys yelling and running off, Lulu dripping blood on him from above. How could he have forgotten all of that?

There was nothing else attached to the memory except vague pain and fear, though it was all mixed up with a terrible loneliness, which might explain why he was so choked up at the sight of his house. It was like he'd been away for a long time though everything was exactly where it was supposed to be. His mother's many plants fought for space with the barbecue and three bicycles, leaving the usual narrow path to the front door.

"I feel like I'm asleep and dreaming."

Not dream.

Lulu was waiting by the door, prancing and wagging her tail, happy to be home. Riley stared at his dog in the glare of the porch light, confused because though he remembered her as old and feeble, this young and fit Lulu seemed normal to him.

Chicken for dinner!

"Dinner?" Riley shook his head and checked his watch but it must have taken a few hits too in that fight because the date and time were wrong. The seconds were still ticking over so it might not be completely broken, just shaken up, like he was.

Open door.

"But what was that light?"

Riley forget.

Lulu turned to the door. She scratched it.

Open door.

Riley sighed and trudged up the stairs. He opened the door and Lulu rushed in excitedly, barking to announce their arrival. They'd had the same routine since he was little, but it felt weird because Lulu was acting almost like a puppy again while

Riley was pretty sure he wasn't five years old anymore.

He bent and managed to unlace his boots even with his awkward and clumsy left hand. It wasn't until he'd wrenched them off that he realized how squeezed and cramped his feet had been. He wiggled his toes and wondered if he'd grabbed someone else's boots by mistake, though he didn't think it was gym day.

Smell chicken.

"I know. It smells amazing." Riley hung his backpack on its hook, still not sure he wasn't dreaming, and unzipped his jacket. He took a hesitant step toward the kitchen and when his dad came around the corner Riley gave him a crushing hug.

"Whoa, son," Dad said, laughing and thumping Riley's back, "Careful you don't break your old man."

Riley pulled back and his smile faltered. They were eye-to-eye, exactly the same height. His dad had been teasing him for weeks, saying that pretty soon Riley would hit a growth spurt and shoot up past him. Riley ducked his head and slouched, taking off his jacket.

"What's for dinner?" he asked in a choked voice. He glanced at Lulu but she was busy sniffing the jumble of shoes and boots under the hallway bench.

"Chicken Cacciatore," Dad said and rubbed his hands together in anticipation. He eyed Lulu appraisingly. "Your dog's looking well today, Riley. That hip might not be as bad as the vet thought."

Lulu's ears twitched and she sat, leaned on the wall and slumped to the left. She wagged her tail and whined when Riley's father patted her head on his way into the kitchen.

Dad not know.

Riley trailed behind him and raised an eyebrow at Lulu. "I don't know either." He barely voiced the thought but felt Lulu acknowledge it in his mind with a burst of doggy love that was intense and almost physical. At least she didn't give him the urge to pee again. He sensed her amusement at that memory. His dog was clearly more clued-in to the situation than he was.

Riley forget.

"Yeah, you said that already. I'm guessing I forgot a lot more than just a bright light."

Lulu rolled to her feet awkwardly and followed him down the hall to the kitchen with drooping ears and a fake limp. She had a drink from her water bowl and curled up on the back door mat to keep her eye on everyone, same as always.

"Have you washed your hands?" Riley's mother called from the stove.

Riley's heart nearly exploded at the sound of his mom's voice, and he would have hugged her if she hadn't been carrying a steaming casserole dish to the table at that moment. He went to the sink instead and washed his hands, grinning and just happy to be home. He watched his mom as he dried his hands, thinking that she was still prettier than any girl he knew.

"I made your favourite tonight," she said and turned to face him. "My goodness, Riley! Do I have to take you shopping again so soon?" She shook her finger at him in mock anger.

"I'm the same guy I was last night," he said weakly, using his dad's corniest line to make her roll her eyes away instead of looking at him too closely.

She swatted his arm and went back to the stove. "You're almost as big as your father. There's a box of his old clothes at the back of our closet you might want to dig through."

"Beverly!" Riley's dad dropped a handful of cutlery to the table with a clatter. "You know that box has some of my favourite shirts in it."

"Don't you use your teacher voice on me, Peter Mason. You haven't been able to button those shirts past your navel for years."

Riley leaned against the counter, listening to his parents as they set the table for supper. Everything was so normal. Nothing had changed yet something had clearly happened to him and Lulu – how else could he be as tall as his dad? He glanced down at pant legs that were much shorter than he would ever wear.

Riley checked his watch again. It was still stuck on July, but *was* working, showing ten minutes had passed since he'd last looked. He glanced at the calendar on the kitchen wall. November, showing a bare forest with snow-capped mountains in the background. Riley ran the math – 241 days. Not possible. He'd know if he was gone that long. Wouldn't he?

But he was wearing clothes that he'd clearly outgrown, and had peeled off boots that he would not be wearing again.

"Riley, bring the salad on your way in," his mom called out from the dining room.

The wooden bowl was wide and shallow, with a flat bottom, and Riley was able to balance it on his left hand with his right arm cradled around it. He managed to slide it onto the table without dumping salad everywhere.

Riley took his seat and kept his left hand on his lap. It would be awkward eating with his right but his father would have too many questions if he saw his misshapen fingers. Questions Riley couldn't yet answer.

Dinner smelled amazing and Riley was practically drooling onto his plate. A little voice at the back of his mind wondered if it had been 241 days since he'd last eaten chicken. Riley gave himself a mental shake and picked up his fork. He was bemused to find that he handled it as if he'd always eaten with that hand, and happily shoveled the savoury chicken as fast as he could chew.

Lulu sat on the floor by his chair and slurped bits of meat from his fingers when he managed to sneak them to her without Mom seeing.

"We should order your birthday cake soon," she said to him between bites. She leaned closer and peered at him. "Weren't you supposed to get a haircut?"

"Birthday? Haircut? Didn't I just…" Riley slouched in his chair and ran a hand through his shaggy brown hair. He thought he remembered a shaved head but had no clue what memories he could trust.

"Sixteen is a landmark birthday and should be celebrated with flair." His mom waved her fork before spearing it into her salad. "What flavour would you like? I'll still get the big cake. I know you don't want a party but you could invite a couple of friends over for dinner."

Riley raised an eyebrow at Lulu. "Chocolate or vanilla?"

Tell Mom chicken.

"I'm not telling Mom I want a chicken cake." Riley laughed inwardly. Talking to Lulu in his head was weird but easy, like they'd been talking this way for a while.

Meatloaf.

"I don't think so." He went back to his dinner and the room turned with him as he moved his head. A nauseating lurch rolled through his gut in response to the motion. He sat very still and the dizziness eased, though his chicken didn't smell so delicious all of a sudden. Riley put down his fork and reached for his water glass.

His mom had stopped talking and he realized they were both staring at him. They were also swaying side to side, like sea grass in a current. Riley was getting dizzy again. He blinked rapidly until they stopped moving.

His father narrowed his eyes, and Riley knew there would be questions later. He was a cool guy but took his dad role really seriously. Riley needed some time to think, to sort out his muddled thoughts and find his own answers first. He looked at his mom, whose expression was clearly expecting a different sort of answer.

"Chocolate," he murmured.

As he expected, his mom went back to her dinner, but just saying the word *chocolate* had doubled his nausea. He swallowed hard and did his best to avoid meeting his dad's questioning gaze.

Little Sister

Day 1

Riley moaned as he regained consciousness. He was freezing. His whole body shivered uncontrollably, just like that one time he'd gone camping in winter. Except for his left hand. It was the only warm spot on his body and it ached dully in a rhythmic pulse timed to his heartbeat. He thought it should hurt a lot more, considering how badly it had been smashed, but someone must have given him drugs to dull the pain.

He breathed shallowly, restricted by his tightly bound ribs, and wondered where Lulu was. She'd been hauled up first and whisked away before Riley was pulled in and dumped roughly on a cold metal floor. He'd cried out in pain and someone shoved him, hard. He'd kept quiet after that. Someone closed the door and the searing light had cut off, throwing Riley into an abrupt darkness that was just as brutal on his abused senses as a punch in the face. Then he'd passed out again.

Riley felt a thrumming vibration through the thin mattress he lay on. Not the rhythmic whump-whump he associated with helicopters, but a steady drone that was more like a plane. Riley didn't care which one it was but only hoped the trip would be short enough to stave off the motion sickness he was already starting to feel. He hated traveling in anything faster than a bicycle, and even that sometimes unsettled him.

Riley opened his eyes to an overhead spotlight that was almost like a sledgehammer. He squinted and swallowed hard, ignoring a twinge of nausea as the head of his bed slowly tilted upward.

He heard movement in the room but was still too blinded to see much past the tiny blanket that covered his torso but left his bare arms and legs sticking out. No wonder he was freezing. He blinked and strained to see in the glaring light, though his left eye tinted everything red and ached dully.

A bulky bandage covered his left hand and secured it to a long narrow board. His right was hidden in a hard metal tube that looked like a mini Quonset hut. It hummed gently, and had a row of yellow lights that blinked randomly. Riley couldn't move his fingers and they were tingly, as if he'd slept on his hand and the feeling was just coming back. He tried to pull his hand out of the tube, and felt a sharp prick on his thumb that sent that tingle rushing up his arm. It was soon as paralyzed as the hand.

"Is anyone there?" The barely whispered words ended in a whimper. His whole face hurt and his jaw creaked when he spoke but nothing else seemed broken – except his nose, which shifted uncomfortably and felt stuffed full of cotton so he couldn't breathe through it.

A damp snout pressed against the inside of Riley's ear and sniffed deeply. It was incredibly loud in his muddled brain and he turned away. A rumbling growl and the nose moved to his neck, sniffing his skin and then into his hair. He felt a velvety tongue behind his ear and then sharp teeth nipped his scalp and yanked out several hairs.

"Ow!"

Someone put a warm, calming hand on Riley's shoulder. He turned his head and saw a lab-coated figure standing next to the bed. He tried to pull away but the hand pressed him back to the mattress.

"Where am I?" he asked, his voice still no more than a raspy whisper.

I am Mirt. You must not move.

Riley went very still, not because he'd been told to but because no one had actually spoken aloud. The words had appeared in his mind while his ears heard only grunting and growls.

"What's going on?"

You are safe and were only slightly damaged.

"I don't understand," Riley said with rising panic. "How am I hearing you in my head?" There were many sounds in the room around him: a rushing hiss that was probably air conditioning, several beeps and clicks and whirs from the machine covering his right hand, and the heavy breathing of the doctor standing next to him.

His ears weren't plugged or covered so the voice was definitely not coming from a headset or ear buds. It was definitely in his head, just talking to him, louder than his own thoughts so he knew he wasn't making it up.

Your blood has been enriched with a compound to enhance the communication process.

"What did you do to me? I thought you were a doctor. Turn it off!" Riley struggled, managing only to hurt himself as he jarred his injuries. "Did anyone call my parents?"

Be quiet or Ruk will sedate you.

Another figure appeared near Riley's feet and moved into his line of sight. He realized what he'd assumed was a white lab coat was really a sort of light brown vest. Whoever Ruk was, he had the hairiest arms Riley had ever seen, and he blinked tears away from his right eye so he could focus.

Riley wished he hadn't. A hairy face straight out of a monster comic loomed over him. It had a long snout ending in large quivering nostrils, and tufted ears that pointed straight at him. The creature jabbed several buttons on the tube that concealed Riley's right hand. It began to beep faster, and more yellow lights winked on.

Now you will sleep and your pains will ease.

"No, please don't!"

The warm tingle was rushing over Riley's shoulder and flooding the rest of his body. His muscles were starting to get heavy and it was taking a huge effort to move any part of his body, including his tongue.

"Where...Lulu..."

The little sister will live.

Seasick

Riley moaned as another wave of nausea rolled through him. It was milder than the last one and he breathed shallowly until it passed. He reached for the glass of water on the bedside table and took a cautious sip. It stayed down.

"My bed feels too soft, like I'm floating in it," he complained. He threw the extra pillow to the foot of the bed, where Lulu lay sprawled near his feet. She took the corner of the pillow between her teeth, pulled it closer and settled her chin on it with a satisfied groan.

Bed good.

There was a light tap at the door and his mother came into the room. She pressed a cool hand to Riley's forehead. "You're not feverish," she said, stroking his cheek. "Can I bring you anything at all?"

"No thanks, Mom. I still feel too sick to eat." Riley kept the blanket pulled up to his chin, and his left hand hidden.

He wanted to throw his arms around her neck, like he'd missed her forever, but she was acting like everything was normal. Which it wasn't – not for Riley, anyway.

His mom moved his water glass closer and picked up several crumpled bits of paper and used tissues from his bedside table and tossed them into the empty waste basket.

"Do you remember that boat we rented when you were eleven? Your father teased you the whole time about leaving your sea legs home." She fussed with his blanket. "You had the same look about you."

"Don't remind me." Riley groaned. That was the worst trip ever. He'd been sick not only the entire four-day trip, but for another two whole days after they got home. They'd never taken another boat trip but his parents still planned a holiday every summer. Riley had gotten used to spending them mostly asleep, stretched out on the car's back seat so he didn't have to look at the moving scenery. His dad had promised him that would change once he got his learner's permit because he'd never heard of anyone complaining of motion sickness while they were driving. That day couldn't come soon enough, as far as Riley was concerned.

His dad watched from the doorway with his hands in his pockets. "Let him rest, Bev," he said quietly.

"A sick boy needs his mother."

"I'm not a boy, Mom." Riley's eyes flicked between his parents. He knew his mother would stay at his side if he asked but his dad was watching Lulu, who was licking a paw. Riley hoped he couldn't see her shorter fangs.

"I'm sure I'll be fine by morning."

"Well, you call out if you need anything," his mom said, stroking his cheek again before leaving the room.

His dad lingered a few moments longer. "Is there anything you want to talk about, Riley?"

"No, Dad." Riley was unable to meet his father's searching gaze. How could he explain that he wasn't sure if he was the same person he'd been when he got up this morning?

His dad sighed and closed the door. Riley knew that sigh. This wasn't over, and there would be questions later. He just hoped he'd be able to answer them.

"I think Mom is right," Riley muttered. "I feel sick, but not from the chicken, more like I've been on a road trip. We weren't in a car or bus at all today, were we?"

On ship.

"I don't remember any stupid ship. You know I hate boats," he said miserably. "I don't even remember going to school this morning."

Lulu laid her snout on her paws and snorted.

Riley forget.

"Yeah, don't you think I know that? Mom and Dad are acting like they saw us just this morning, like it's been a normal school day, but I feel like today wasn't so normal." He sat up, feeling weak and unsteady. "What if you're right? What if there's nothing wrong with my watch? What if I'm not crazy? What if we really *were* gone 241 days?"

Not days. Always night.

"Whatever." Riley squeezed his eyes shut and took a couple of deep breaths. He tried to guess at what Lulu wasn't able to explain. She might seem smarter than usual, but she still lived in the here-and-now with little concept of time, like any dog. He was lucky to have the watch and not have to rely on Lulu to tell him how long they'd been away – if that's what had really happened.

He reached for the water again with a steadier hand, though his fingers barely folded around the glass. He didn't think his parents had seen his bent fingers, but his dad didn't miss much and might have noted Riley eating with his right hand, an oddity.

Earlier, his parents had chatted about the usual everyday stuff while Riley wolfed down the most delicious dinner he could remember ever having. When the room had started to spin, he'd barely made it upstairs to the bathroom before vomiting everything he'd eaten. He'd retched long after there was anything left to bring up and then had lain on the floor with his face pressed against the cool tile while his worried mother called from the hallway.

When he managed to get up and wash his face he'd been shocked at the image in the mirror. His hair was shaggy and longer than he usually kept it. His arms and chest were bigger, his muscles more defined. And he was definitely taller.

There were two black streaks on the mirror, at chin level. He'd reached out to wipe them off when he noticed the marker sitting at the edge of the sink, and vaguely remembered drawing a mustache on his reflection. He'd bent his knees to bring his face down a couple of inches, placing the marker-mustache under his nose. He'd then stood straight and the mustache dropped to his chin again, like a scrawny beard.

He had felt a sick dread, knowing full well that those marks wouldn't have lasted more than a couple of days before his mother came along and wiped the mirror clean. He'd swiped a hand across the marks, smearing the glass.

"Nothing here has changed but it all looks and feels odd, except for you," he said, reaching for Lulu. "You're completely different but somehow feel more normal than anything else in this room."

Lulu nuzzled his hand and crawled closer so he could scratch behind her ears.

"The white fur is gone from your face. Your eyes aren't cloudy. You've lost your limp. If we've been gone long enough for me to get older, how is it you look like you went backwards in time?"

Mirt fix.

"Yeah, sure maybe someone fixed your blurry eyes and gimpy leg but how did your fur get thick and shiny again? And you look younger. You act it too."

Lulu young.

She rolled over and Riley stroked her silky belly fur.

"Dad was watching you with his teacher face. He knows something's up. You have to slow down around him until we figure out what's happened. Dad's gonna notice pretty soon that we're different, and that I'm as tall as he is now. Do you get that?"

Riley grow.

"Yeah, I grow, I mean grew. That didn't happen in one day. Even my face looks different. When I look in the mirror it's like I'm seeing one of the seniors at school." He stopped short and realized he'd have to go to school in the morning. He wondered if anyone would notice that he'd changed. Maybe they'd be oblivious, like his mother, but Matt and the twins were always looking for a reason to torment him and would expect him to be mangled and bruised.

He inspected his scarred fingers. If his parents hadn't changed and he was as tall as his dad, he should be taller than those guys now. School might be interesting tomorrow.

He looked around his room, at the posters of bands whose songs he could hardly remember, and at the computer sitting on his desk. He knew it was protected by a password but he had no idea what it was, only that he changed it frequently so his parents couldn't snoop. The room felt weird, like none of this stuff was his even though he knew it was.

"I'm getting used to hearing you in my head. It feels almost normal, like we've been talking like this for a long time."

Lulu talk.

"Good thing, since somehow I've forgotten a huge chunk of something weird." He wondered if he'd ever remember, though when Lulu had mentioned the bright light the memory had been there, like he'd just needed reminding.

Lulu remember.

"Okay, tell me something else I've forgotten, like, did I have any friends?"

Ruk friend.

"What's a ruk-friend?"

Lulu poked him with her snout.

Ruk friend.

Closer Is Louder

Day 5

Riley tried the door again. Still locked. He paced the length of the room to keep warm. Three long strides and turn, back and forth like a tiger in a cage. He'd been locked in since leaving the medical bay a day ago. On the short walk through a cold hallway he'd glimpsed a stunning view through a small round window – pinpricks of light in the distance, some streaking past as if they were closer, all on a background of deep black. That's when he'd finally accepted the reality that he was on a spaceship headed for an alien planet.

He wasn't sure how long he'd been on board but it had to be at least a week – a week without news of Lulu, only that she was alive and in some kind of stasis chamber.

He had explored every inch of his cell – several times. Other than the locked door, the room held nothing but a thin mat with a coarse blanket and a hole in one corner where he could squat. There were no windows, only slits in the walls for ventilation. One blasted the side of his neck with cold air as he stalked past and he shivered as he ducked his head.

Riley reached for the blanket on the mat but his bandaged ribs wouldn't allow him to bend over far enough. He put his back to the wall and slid partway down until he could grab the blanket, but just bracing his muscles to slide back up again sent pain lancing through his chest. He closed his eyes and breathed shallowly until it subsided, then slumped all the way down onto the mat.

He awkwardly wrapped the blanket around his shoulders, careful not to jar his loosely splinted left hand. He worried that the fingers would not heal properly. They'd taken no x-rays and, when he'd asked about it, Ruk said that his bones were more complex that theirs. Riley wondered what could be more complex than alien fingers with extra joints that bent both ways.

At least the nausea was gone. Travelling in cars and boats had always made him sick. Apparently, so did spaceships. He huddled on the mat, shivering in his thin blanket. He wanted to go home, to be in his own bed with his mom nursing him back to health instead of in this cold room. He wanted a real doctor – a human doctor.

Riley's left eye still filtered everything through a reddish haze but he could now open it all the way without feeling like it was being stabbed by a fork. His head still hurt from the battering it took, but now also pulsed with a muted babble that was like wearing cheap earplugs in a room jammed with people all talking at once. Ruk said that he'd eventually learn to hear only the voices he was meant to be listening to.

Ruk was the only alien that Riley had seen up close – besides the medic, Mirt. They were like midget werewolves, with rounded ears and pointed snouts. Their fur was very short and bristly, and they wore a sort of coverall and stubby boots that looked metallic but hardly made a sound as they walked.

He'd spotted a few others, mostly staring at him from across the room when he was still strapped to a bed in the medical bay. They were nearly a head taller than Ruk and Mirt, with shorter snouts and louder voices. Riley hadn't liked the look of them, as they scowled and bared their teeth at him, though he'd been drugged and might have only imagined they were sizing him up for their next meal.

Riley ran a hand over his stubbly scalp. He'd woken up at some point shaved all over and flea-dipped. He could still smell its acrid stink on his skin. Ruk had apologized, said it was a precaution they were obliged to take when they brought alien organisms aboard. Riley was so surprised that these aliens saw *him* as an alien that he'd forgotten to complain.

I bring food. Stand away.

The words were loud and clear in his head, and drowned out all the other voices. Riley couldn't decide which was more oppressive, the constant crowd muttering at the edges of his thoughts or Ruk's insistent messages that appeared without warning.

Riley's stomach growled at the mention of food. He hated the slop they gave him to eat but he was starving and they only fed him once a day. He also hated knowing about the additive in the food that kept him linked to their stupid hive mind, if that's what it was. When he'd threatened to go on a hunger strike so he could shut them out of his head, Ruk gave him the choice of eating his meal or being restrained for a shot.

Being abducted by aliens wasn't nearly as cool as people imagined.

His mom would be freaking out by now and sending his dad out to search the woods again and again, even though the police would already have done that with dogs. She'd stay glued to the phone at home, keeping constant contact by text with his dad. Riley hadn't seen *his* phone but probably couldn't get a signal out here anyway. Wherever *here* was.

The latch released and the door scraped across the floor. Ruk stepped in and shoved the door shut. Riley knew it would lock automatically. Ruk handed him a bowl and scooper. Riley sighed, even as he dug in hungrily. He told himself it was pea soup with croutons but it tasted more like chunks of clay floating in sour porridge.

He watched Ruk while he ate his gloopy, chewy meal. The alien waited by the door in a half-crouch, watching Riley eat. His black snout was streaked with white in a pattern similar to Lulu's, possibly marking Ruk as old – though Riley hadn't met enough aliens to compare.

Why did those others punish you?

"What makes you think they were punishing me? Maybe they're just jerks who like to hurt people."

Your people harm each other for pleasure?

Riley sighed. "They made me steal a test from my father. It wasn't the first time and I wanted to teach them a lesson, I guess. I filled it out with wrong answers and they all failed." He wondered if his dad knew by now that he'd stolen the test. He might have talked to everyone who failed but Riley didn't think any of them would admit to cheating, though Adam might tell if he thought it would help the search for his friend.

Ruk regarded him solemnly with his head tilted to the left. It reminded him of Lulu when she was confused.

"Am I a prisoner?" Riley asked, changing the subject.

Ruk shifted his position, shuffling his short legs until his back rested against the wall. He grunted as he settled on his haunches. His powerful arms hung limply, with his three-fingered hands on the floor.

This is quarantine. You know this.

Riley swallowed the last bite and set the bowl on the floor. "All I know is you've locked me in a room. Am I kidnapped or arrested?" He struggled to his feet, determined to get some answers. "I've already been in here for days, I don't know where I am, and my parents probably think I'm dead."

We saved you and the little sister. We will fix you both and take you home.

"You call this *saving?*" Riley shouted. He leaned over Ruk, who looked small crouched next to the door. Riley knew his size was deceiving. Ruk could easily pick him up and restrain him. His claws were sharp and he had nipped Riley with those teeth a few times already to keep him away from the door.

Ruk jabbered and growled out loud as he answered in Riley's mind.

Thinking voice and speaking voice are loud together.

Riley grimaced at Ruk's amplified internal voice and lowered his own. "Okay, okay, I know. You don't need me yelling gibberish at you when you're getting an instant translation. Sorry."

Shouting does not make more understanding.

"What about Lulu? We know a lot of each other's...um...words. I mean, I talk and she barks but we mostly communicate about only a few things. Will her thoughts translate in my head too?"

She has the serum and it may work.

"You mean if she lives," Riley said glumly and slumped against the wall. "She's kind of old to survive a beating like that."

I have told you the little sister will live.

"Why do you keep calling Lulu my little sister?"

Ruk tilted his head again. *She is not* your *little sister.*

Riley was afraid to ask what that meant. "How much longer until we reach your planet?" Ruk and Mirt had told him that Lulu needed urgent care that could only be provided on their home planet, which they called Metarra. Riley would have preferred a vet for Lulu but he was just grateful they were keeping her alive.

We approach the median.

"Where's that?"

The median is the space between two places and we are nearly there.

Riley frowned at Ruk. "You mean we're only half way there? We've been on your stupid ship almost a week already. That'll mean a whole month before we get home!"

There is time. It will be done.

Ruk gestured at Riley's left hand. Riley opened his mouth to say no but Ruk grunted in that manner that usually preceded force, so he obeyed and gingerly pulled his bandaged hand out of its sling. Riley tried not to whimper as Ruk unwrapped his hand. The medical bay had an assortment of splinting devices shaped for Metarran hands and Mirt had tried several on Riley before sending several assistants on errands. They'd returned with a variety of shaped metal pieces, none of which quite fit.

Riley winced at the sight of his swollen fingers. They looked like lumpy grey sausages. "That doc hasn't looked at any of my injuries for days. How can you be sure I'm healing okay?"

Mirt tends to greater injuries than yours.

Riley hissed in pain as Ruk inspected the damaged fingers. The alien was surprisingly gentle as he adjusted the delicate splints with hands that were blocky and strong, his fingers and thumb twice as thick as Riley's.

How does your head feel?

"It hurt a lot less after you got here," Riley said. "Before that, I swear I could hear everyone on the ship, but couldn't make out what they were saying."

You will hear when others talk or think of you.

"I don't hear them talking. It's just a lot of noise."

Closer is louder. Listen to me and others disappear. Easiest if you don't speak aloud at all.

"I can't have a conversation with you without saying the words out loud, even if I sound like I'm talking to myself all the time."

You cannot hear if you only talk.

Ruk helped slide his hand back in the improvised sling and adjusted the bandage that bound Riley's chest.

"I'm gonna go crazy if I have to sit in here all the time," Riley said. "What do Metarrans do for fun?"

Ruk stood to his full height, which brought the top of his head barely above Riley's elbow. He stretched his long arms over his head and then brought them down swiftly, using his oddly-jointed fingers to propel himself along the floor to the door with astonishing speed.

Metarrans run.

Itchy Butt

Riley stood under the shower for a long time. It felt amazing, maybe the best ever, the hot water clearing the last of the dizziness. He hadn't slept well. Lulu had jumped off the bed a half dozen times in the night, scratching and pacing and muttering about her itchy butt.

He'd had weird dreams – when he managed to sleep – but he couldn't remember any details after he woke up until the shower spray hit his face and he recalled climbing out of a pool of tepid water where a dozen furred creatures lounged and bathed. Clots of fur floated on the surface and stuck to his skin. The memory even carried the scent of wet animal.

The thick towel he used to dry off felt like a luxury and triggered another dream fragment: standing naked on a cold floor, drying off with his t-shirt only to be soaked again when the creatures shook the water from their fur. He felt a nudge behind his knee and looked down into Lulu's clear brown eyes.

"Everything is just too weird." Riley scratched her forehead.

Remember ship?

"Sorry, Lulu. I still don't remember any kind of ship." He swiped at the steamed mirror and peered at his reflection, noting that his cheeks and chin were more defined, sharper, like his father's face. It was both strange and familiar. "But something sure as hell *did* happen to us."

Bright light.

Riley shuddered and tightened the towel around his waist. "Don't remind me. It was probably some sort of military radioactive beam that cooked us while we were lying unconscious in the grass. The healing was only a side-effect that we won't get to enjoy anyway because we'll soon die of radiation poisoning."

Lulu rolled her eyes and trotted back to his room.

"I know, I know," he said, following her. "Healing our bones instantly is one thing, but how did I get older without any memory of time passing? And you're young, like a whole different dog."

Same dog.

"It just seems impossible that we could be gone almost a whole year and not even an hour passed for everyone else." Riley picked up the clothes he'd tossed on a chair last night and emptied his pockets. "It's like we're stuck in a bad B-movie. I've lost my memory and only my dog knows what's going on."

He pulled out his wallet and checked his student card. The photo was of a younger Riley, though it showed the same year as the calendar in the kitchen.

Stay home.

"I'd like to but Dad would hear about it right away." Until he figured out what was happening, he needed to act normal. That meant going to school, just like any other day.

Riley turned a pocket inside out and picked Lulu's bloodied and broken teeth away from the fabric. He cupped them in his palm to let her have a sniff. She growled and backed away.

Lulu teeth.

"The blood's barely dried." Riley dropped them into a jar of pennies and shook it a few times to mix them in. The coppery tang from the coins would mask any lingering bloody scent. He might want to look at them again later.

There was a drawstring pouch in the other front pocket of his jeans. It held a handful of coarse grey powder.

Special food.

"This is how I hear you in my head?" Riley dipped a finger and tasted. It was chalky and bland. "There isn't much. How do we use it?"

Lulu shook her head and sneezed. *Ruk say how.*

"I don't remember Ruk so I won't remember anything he said." Riley closed the pouch and shoved it far under his mattress. He didn't want his parents to find it and assume he was taking drugs. He wouldn't be able to hide his confusion if they questioned him closely. They'd think he was high.

Lulu jumped off the bed and snapped at her hind end, spinning in place but not quite reaching. She bumped Riley's desk and his lamp teetered.

"Hey, quit fooling around."

Itchy butt.

Riley steadied the lamp. "You'd better not have fleas again. Dad will give you that bath you hate." He threw his jeans into a corner. They'd been uncomfortably tight when he got home last night. He went through his entire closet and found that all his pants were too tight, and too short. Same for most of his shirts.

Riley bigger.

"Yeah, I'm bigger," Riley said and sat on his bed. "I'm taller and wider and the only things that fit are my bathrobe and some bright yellow sweat pants." He frowned at the pile of clothing in the corner. "I'm going to look like a dork."

Wear man clothes.

Riley blinked at Lulu several times. He couldn't decide whether Lulu had understood his mom when she mentioned the box of clothes during dinner last night or if Lulu now saw Riley as man-sized.

"You're right, but Dad's clothes are guaranteed to be dorkier."

Riley peered out into the hall, checking for his parents. He didn't really expect to run into them, since they usually left the house a full hour before he did, but this was no ordinary morning and he wasn't taking any chances.

His parents' room faced east and sunlight streamed through the sheer curtains. The clock showed that his first class started in twenty minutes. It would take that long just to get there – if he ran. He was going to be late.

There were several stacked boxes at the back of his parents' closet. All but one bore his mother's name in black marker. Riley maneuvered out his dad's box and carried it to his room. He dumped the contents onto his bed. The clothes smelled like his father, and reminded him that no time had really passed here and, if the kitchen calendar was right, he had stolen that history test only yesterday. Riley's face flushed, but his regret about stealing the test felt old, as if he'd gotten over it long ago.

Lulu poked through the mound of clothing, sniffing and snorting.

Man clothes.

"Hey! Don't slobber everything," Riley said, pushing her away. He tossed all the loud shirts and dress pants – his dad's teacher clothes – back into the box, and was left with two pairs of jeans, a faded green flannel shirt, and a brown leather belt.

The jeans were a bit loose but perfect for tucking in a flannel shirt. Riley buckled the belt and turned to Lulu with raised eyebrows. "They're not much different from what I wear every day, though maybe a little more retro than my usual style." She gave him a wide doggy grin and panted.

Riley checked the effect in his mother's full-length mirror. He felt weird in his father's clothes, as if he were a little kid playing dress-up. He glanced at a photo on his mother's bedside table. He'd been only three years old when it was taken. His father was wearing the same green shirt that Riley had on and it emphasized the resemblance between them.

At least it all fits, he thought, as he went back into the closet for shoes. Not so lucky, as he had to settle for scuffed brown loafers, but at least his toes wouldn't be jammed together all day.

Lulu's Riley

Day 12

Riley lay awake in the dark. He could hear humming, or at least what the Metarran version of humming sounded like to him, a sort of gargling and groaning. The same five notes, looped over and over, signaled to Riley that Ruk was on his way.

The light came on in the room and Riley struggled to the edge of his cot, blinded and bleary-eyed. He wasn't hungry so it couldn't be morning, though now that he was getting two meals a day he sometimes slept-in until his breakfast showed up.

Ruk nodded when he saw Riley awake.

The little sister has returned.

That got Riley's attention and cleared his head. "Lulu's back on the ship? Is she okay?" Ruk's expression soured and Riley realized he'd been yelling out loud. Again. He crouched a little to show Ruk he was sorry, and bit his lips to keep quiet. "Are we going home now? How long till we reach Earth?"

Now we seek again. It is not the same as returning.

"What does that mean?" Riley snatched up a blanket from his mat, the one with a hole torn in the centre that he wore as a poncho when he wasn't sleeping.

The blood that you and the little sister left on the ground of your planet will guide our direction.

Ruk hurried through the chilly hallways, knowing that Riley would follow. Riley's lungs were still restricted by his bound chest and he was soon panting but felt better than the last time he'd left his cell.

Every morning after breakfast, Ruk took him to a wide corridor that followed along the inside of the ship's outer hull. It was a very popular corridor and most crewmembers ran it at least once a day, some circling the track in a meditative jog while others raced past in an endless complex competition.

Riley couldn't move faster than a shuffle the first time and he ached for hours afterward. By the third day he was moving more smoothly – if still not quickly – and now looked forward to his daily exercise, but mostly to get out of his cell.

It was hard not to stop at every porthole to stare at the billions of lights moving past, a completely different sky every time he looked. He hadn't seen much else of the ship beyond the running track – and the long stinking room he'd nicknamed Pee Park – but he'd met more of the crew in the few times he'd been allowed out. There were twelve others like Ruk, called Alphas, and six of the taller loud ones that Ruk called Scouts. He said the Scouts were a sort of hybrid, a lower caste of Metarran. Riley had noticed how the other Alphas treated Ruk – one of their own yet kept at a distance – and wondered how many layers and castes their society had.

Ruk stopped when they reached a pair of translucent doors.

She is in Mirt's care.

A bulbous glass dome jutted out of the wall to their right. Its red glow changed to brilliant yellow when Ruk pressed his palm against it, and the doors opened.

Riley tried to push past but Ruk poked him in the back with a claw tip, a clear warning to Riley and one he quickly obeyed.

Speak softly and move slowly.

This was a different medical bay than the one Riley had been in. The lighting was warmer and the empty beds had thicker blankets than he'd been given. The whole place was bigger and cleaner. There was a lot more equipment, weird-looking but obviously medical and more advanced than what was used on him. In comparison, his medical treatment had been more like basic first aid.

Ruk led him to a separate room, smaller and with only one raised cot. Riley's chin quivered at the sight of Lulu strapped to the bed, facing away from the entrance. Silver tubes snaked around her body, leading to various machines that blinked and bleeped. She was very thin and her fur was dull and matted.

This was his fault. If only he'd stood up to those guys and said no – or even told his dad what was happening – Lulu would never have been hurt. He glanced back at Ruk, who nodded and left the room. Riley rounded the cot, careful not to jostle the equipment.

Long metal rods skewered her head and muzzle, forming a cage that kept her jaws still and her teeth slightly apart. Her tongue hung through the rods, panting. Dried blood was caked where the screws met Lulu's skin and at the corners of her mouth, but nothing looked swollen or infected. Her nose twitched in his direction.

"Good girl, good Lulu," Riley murmured to her questioning whine, and touched her nose through the cage so she could sniff him and know he was there. He ran a trembling hand along her back and her tail swished feebly.

Hear Riley. Lulu's Riley.

He continued to stroke her fur, feeling a little less homesick now that he knew she really was alive. It was amazing to hear her voice in his head as clearly as he heard Ruk's, and it closely matched what he'd always thought she'd sound like if she could speak. He squatted next to the cot so she could see his face. Her tail wagged more energetically and Riley scrubbed tears from his cheeks with his good hand.

"Yeah, Lulu's Riley."

Dog House

Lulu stretched her neck and sniffed the breeze flowing over the top of the fence. The wet scent of winter rains coming was the sharpest in her nose, but the rich loamy backdrop of the woods at the end of the road beckoned her with its promise of soft mossy ground under her paws.

It was much better than the scents closer to the ground. She wrinkled her nose at the acrid smell of her own pee, heaviest in the narrow space between the fence and her dog house. It smelled as strong and fresh as any marking she'd left in Pee Park, though this pee reeked of sick and old.

Lulu was confused by this smell that was familiar, hers but not hers. She only vaguely remembered her older self, aware that there'd once been a time when she couldn't run. But she could run now. She raced around the perimeter of the yard several times, digging her claws into the ground for speed as she cornered.

She flopped down, panting, and rolled in the dried grass beneath the tree that Riley used to climb when he was small. She wriggled among the gnarled roots that bulged across the grass, scratching all the itchy places. She jumped to her feet and shook off the bits of grass and dirt, sneezing forcefully.

Lulu spied her ball near the gate and snatched it up. It felt strange in her mouth, different without her fangs, but tasted the same. She flung it against the fence a few times and chased it. She wanted Riley to throw it for her.

Riley school.

She dropped the ball and pushed at the gate. Riley had latched it when he left, making her promise to stay here, and making his own promise to come home at lunch. She didn't think Riley had made it as far as the park before his voice faded completely.

Riley hear Lulu?

She listened intently but didn't hear his voice in response. It was good not to hear nasty comments from the Scouts about Lulu's smell and how stupid she was, but not hearing Riley was unsettling. No matter how far away from her he'd been on the ship, she could at least feel him at the back of her mind.

Her frustrated growl ended in a squeak when the bump under her skin started vibrating again. She reached back to bite it but got only a mouthful of fur. She rolled on the ground, trying to rub the itchy spot, but it hurt where it pressed against the dry grass.

Lulu barked a greeting to the neighbourhood just to make noise and several dogs answered, though none sounded surprised to hear her. They were like Riley's parents and didn't even know she'd been away.

She paced the yard, her paws wanting to cover the short distance to the woods and race to the top of the mossy hill. She vaguely remembered her legs being too weak to make it all the way up but knew now she could run up and down without getting tired.

Lulu sniffed deeply at the loose board at the corner of the fence, another place where her older self's scent was strong. That scent was also on everything in the house, as was Riley's. It was as if she and Riley had never left and been on the ship.

Their scents should have faded while they were away.

Riley forget.

If Riley could remember he would tell her why she could smell them as strongly here as in their room on the ship. She grumbled, feeling as stupid as Kar said she was. Lulu pushed the board aside, flattening her ears at the familiar squeal of the rusty nail that held it to the cross bar. She squeezed her body through the narrow gap and into the laneway that ran along the back of the houses. The board swung back into place with another screech.

She trotted to the end of the laneway to stare at the woods across the wide road. Cars whizzed past from both directions. Lulu hadn't crossed it without Riley since her eyes had dimmed. Now she would run across without fear. Her nose twitched as it filled with rich, moist scents. Even the cars smelled better to her than the stale tang of the ship.

Lulu whined, wanting to race across the road and run in the woods, but she was getting nervous about not hearing Riley in her head. He'd been away from her too long.

Go school.

No Scritches for Bitches

Day 61

Riley stuck his head through the lounge door, checking to see how many Metarrans might be there. He didn't mind the Alphas. They were all old and mostly left him alone as long as he stayed out of trouble. It was the Scouts he wanted to avoid. They were fewer but made up for it by being obnoxious and in-your-face. They barely reached his shoulder and tended to be scrawny but their aggressive natures made them more intimidating than their small size would hint at. It didn't help that they all had tough sharp claws that could easily rip through his skin, and jaws even more powerful than Lulu's.

The lounge was huge, with several communal areas filled with cushions for lying around and a couple of private alcoves that he didn't ever want to go into, judging by the embarrassing sounds he'd heard coming from behind the curtains.

Kar and Pru were at the other end of the room, jabbering in low tones with two other Scouts. Riley had learned to tell them apart – it helped that there were only six of them – and recognized their brother Por and his buddy Trit. He was careful not to make eye contact with Trit or Por, as they would gleefully interpret that as an invitation to remind Riley – again – that *he* was the alien on this ship.

The Scouts' brown eyes and mobile faces were more expressive than the Alphas could manage, and Riley recognized the looks of sour distaste at his and Lulu's presence. He followed Lulu to their favourite spot, where the cushions were relatively clean and they had a clear view of the whole room.

"If I've counted right, today is my sixteenth birthday."

Lulu rolled a skeptical eye to Riley. *No smell cake.*

"Nope, no cake." Cake was the only thing that Lulu liked about birthdays. The rest of it was *too much noise.*

Riley had tried to explain birthdays to Ruk, who compared them to Metarran naming-days though he didn't understand why Riley thought he could celebrate when he hadn't changed his name.

"Pretty soon we'll be home and Mom will be so happy to see us that she'll let us eat cake every day if we want it."

Riley miss Mom.

"Yeah, I miss Mom for sure, and not just because I want a birthday cake." Riley dropped onto the rough cushion next to Lulu, who sighed and settled against him. She rested her chin on Riley's knee.

Lulu miss ball.

"Yeah, it's been a long time since you were strong enough to chase and fetch. I'll see if I can make some sort of ball for you. We can take it to the track at night so none of the others will see, okay?"

Always night.

Riley snorted surprised laughter. "I guess you're right. It's always dark when you're in outer space." He stroked her head and scratched behind one ear, careful to avoid tender spots.

"How's your face feel?"

No hurt. Feel good.

86

The cage had only come off Lulu's head a couple of days ago. It had to hurt – the bolts left six holes in her skull that had yet to heal – but she wasn't about to complain and end up in the medical bay again.

In the couple of months since they'd been on the ship, Riley and Lulu had healed and grown stronger. The bandages were gone and the bruises had faded. Riley clenched his left hand. It closed only part way, not even enough to hold a tennis ball, let alone make a fist.

When Riley's father had fractured his knee there'd been two surgeries, months immobilized in casts, and grueling physiotherapy. His dad hardly limped now but he'd been in the care of several specialists, something Riley wasn't going to get from the Metarrans.

He massaged his stiff fingers, feeling the hard ridges where bony ends had knit together. He didn't know much of anything about healing bones but didn't think his fingers should be crooked and lumpy. The Metarrans' focus had been on saving Lulu's life, and not so much on tending to Riley's few broken bones and bruises.

The black fur on Lulu's face was growing in, filling in the spaces between scars, giving her a mottled snout that bent a couple of degrees to the left. It was missing the sprinkle of white Riley was used to seeing, a change that was minor compared to her clear eyes and energetic walk.

He dug his chilly fingers into the thick fur at her shoulders, finding the stiff muscles that had been holding up Lulu's caged head for two months. His fingers warmed as he kneaded, exercising his hand and loosening Lulu's muscles.

Riley couldn't remember the last time he'd been warm and was jealous that every other being on the ship was furry. When Ruk gave him a stack of old, foul-smelling blankets, Riley washed them and tore the thickest into a couple of long strips that he kept wrapped around his head and neck most days, like a desert nomad.

He and Lulu were allowed about an hour a day in the lounge, though the Metarrans didn't call it an hour. Nothing on the ship appeared to follow any clock-driven schedule that Riley could figure out. Ruk had taught him to recognize a specific grunt that signified a measure of time, dependent on the volume and force of the grunt. So, *We go run GRUNT*, might mean we're going to run in an hour – or six. It might also mean we're going to run *for* an hour – or six.

Riley had taken Lulu to the running track as soon as Mirt allowed it. They had limped together, then walked, and now could run short sprints. With the metal brace off her head, Lulu could now exercise more and regain her strength.

They were also allowed into the water rooms once a day. There were large pools for bathing and a spray room with a separate area for shaking. When Riley complained about all the hair floating in the water, he was given a net and now he skimmed fur out of the pools every afternoon. Disgusting, but he did get first bath when he'd finished cleaning the water. Lulu loved lying in the hottest pool while he cleaned. It helped that most Metarrans found Riley's fur-less skin disturbing and avoided the water rooms if he and Lulu were there.

It made up for how much they both hated nPee Park, which was pungent with the scent markings of every alien on the ship. Lulu always hurried as she sniffed the length of the narrow room for a spot that hadn't been used too recently. Riley still mostly used the hole in the corner of their room.

Not wanting to appear like he was complaining – and get assigned another chore – Riley was careful when he asked Ruk why they all peed in public.

Scent is part of social life, part of community.

At least here in the lounge there were several separate areas and always room for him and Lulu to remain apart from the others. She felt threatened and ridiculed by most of the hybrid Scouts, the males always sniffing and following. The females just wanted her gone, though some had implied that they could use a strong pet. Riley couldn't tell if they meant him or Lulu.

Say stupid.

"You're not stupid, Lulu." Riley glanced across the room, where the two males were leaving.

Kar and Pru say.

"They're just gossiping bitches. Ignore them." He touched Lulu's nose and she licked his hand. Kar and Pru reminded Riley of Jody and Jerry, with the same mean eyes and angry natures. Kar was worse than her sister and took every opportunity to torment Lulu.

Say little sister.

"It's just a nickname." He smiled when he felt her grumble. "We can give them nicknames too. We'll call Kar *Putt-Putt*."

Lulu tilted her head.

"Get it?"

Putt-putt? She looked skeptical.

"Remember when I was little and played with cars? That was the sound I made: putt-putt-putt." Even though his dog was a lot smarter than she was a few months ago, she still didn't get most of his jokes.

Kar-putt-putt?

"No, just Putt-Putt. Like she's a car." The joke was starting to seem lame – even to Riley, who loved corny jokes – and he was about to drop it when Lulu's jaws parted and her tongue lolled out in a full doggy grin.

Kar! Putt-Putt!

She barked loudly and wagged her tail.

Kar and Pru answered just as loudly from across the room, their voices undeniably more aggressive. Kar laid her head on her sister's lap, posing to mimic Lulu. She grabbed Pru's hand, licking and slobbering until they were both hooting with laughter.

Lulu growled but Riley quieted her with a touch. They had agreed she wouldn't respond to the Scouts' taunts but it wasn't easy when Kar and Pru were making such an obvious mockery of Lulu. He scratched her ears and she leaned into his fingers.

No scritches for bitches.

Riley laughed and leaned over to snatch up several more pillows, arranging them around him and Lulu. He still wasn't certain if those guys at the park had given him such a beating that he was actually lying in a coma somewhere, dreaming about being on an alien spaceship with Lulu, who was young again and cracking jokes.

The sisters were heading for the door on all fours, moving with an exaggerated waddle and sniffing everything as they went. They deliberately wagged their tails – which for a Metarran was an aggressive gesture. Their path took them past Lulu, who ignored them, though her fur bristled and she panted anxiously. Riley draped one of his blankets over Lulu's head. She grumbled but settled down.

"If I'm in a coma and this is all a dream," Riley said, wrapping another blanket around his shoulders, "then we might as well relax and have a nap."

Crooked Fingers

Riley paused before opening the classroom door. He gripped the knob with his right hand, automatically, like he'd been doing all morning. He'd been born a lefty but now was favouring his right hand as if he'd been using it long enough to become habit.

He could see someone moving around on the other side of the frosted glass. Riley only vaguely remembered his class schedule and hoped this was the room he was supposed to be in. He took a deep breath, telling himself that his stomach was just nervous and not getting queasy. He'd had to stop twice on the way to school and sit with his head between his knees because the trees and buildings were swaying in time with his footsteps.

Riley wished he'd stayed home with Lulu, but he had to know if Adam and the others had changed too. If they were bigger and older – like him – it might prove they'd all been irradiated in some sort of military training accident, otherwise he'd have to reconsider Lulu's crazy alien abduction story. Either possibility was farfetched, though it sure felt like he'd been away for a long time.

It would explain why everything that *should* be familiar was not, and why he hadn't been able to get into his locker when he finally found it. He'd spun the dial hopefully, but his brain hadn't provided any numbers. No way he'd opened it just yesterday.

The knob turned abruptly and Riley nearly fell into the room when the door swung inward. He kept his left hand hidden in his pocket and slapped on a polite smile.

"Well, if it isn't Mr. Mason," said a thin balding man that Riley recognized as his English teacher.

"Please, do grace us with your presence," Mr. Breen continued as he stepped aside and bowed Riley into the room. A few snickers rose in the packed classroom as Riley hurried to the only empty seat, next to Adam.

His chest tightened with conflicting emotions: happy to see his best friend, hurt and angry at being betrayed. His breath hitched and as he turned away to slide off his backpack the room began to tilt, like the buildings and trees outside but without the nausea.

Riley dropped into his chair as a sudden heat rushed through his whole body and he remembered… EVERYTHING! The memories were just there, like they'd never been gone. He *had* been away for eight months, flying in a space ship to another planet and back. How could he forget all that? He couldn't wait to tell Lulu that he finally understood what she'd been trying to tell him. Riley nearly laughed out loud at how his ridiculous military-accident–irradiation theory didn't sound so crazy next to the truth.

He set his pack on the floor between his feet, and smiled tentatively at Adam, who stared back while leaning as far away from Riley as possible. Riley's smile faltered as he took in the expression on Adam's face.

There was fear. There was awe and disbelief. There was a massive bruise and a red film over Adam's eye. Riley knew how that felt, seeing through a hazy red tint. He brought a hand up to touch the corner of his own eye and Adam's stare shifted to Riley's hand. His mouth opened, as if to speak, then he clapped it shut and turned in his seat to face toward the front of the class.

Adam stared at the clock over the blackboard, willing himself not to turn around. He hadn't slept all night, unable to shake the image of Riley's face when his hand was crushed. Riley's hand sure didn't look broken now, though Adam had not only felt the bones break under his heel but heard their wet crunch.

Matt said they were only going to confront Riley about the test, shake him up a little. Adam should have known the twins wouldn't just want to talk. He tried to tell them to stop but Jody twisted his arm practically out of its socket. It hurt so much he could barely breathe so he'd hammered his foot down as hard as he could and Jody let him go.

Riley watched Adam twitching as if he needed to turn around. Normally they'd be passing notes by now, making plans for after school. But normal had taken a turn for the weird 241 days ago even though for Adam it had only happened last night.

"Mr. Mason? Your homework?"

Riley's head snapped forward and he gaped at Mr. Breen. Homework?

"Need I remind you that your final mark depends on this essay?" Mr. Breen crossed his arms and nodded at the pile of papers on his desk.

Riley pawed through his backpack but saw nothing that looked like an essay. He barely remembered writing one, though as far as anyone else in the room knew he had waited until the last minute like most of them and finished it just last night. His head was spinning and he couldn't make sense of the jumble of books and candy wrappers in his pack.

A hand snaked over from the desk behind his. Tina pulled a sheaf of stapled pages from between two textbooks and unfolded them. Riley bit back a hysterical laugh as he took the pages from Tina, recognizing his handwriting but little else. He nodded thanks and saw her eyes widen in surprise when they met his.

Riley took the unfamiliar homework to the front of the class and presented it with a flourish. Mr. Breen accepted it with a pinched expression that seemed more puzzled than angry. Riley hunched – suddenly feeling too tall – and hurried back to his seat.

Mr. Breen followed him bemusedly, watched him slump into his seat. His students sometimes sprouted inches overnight, transformed from child to adult over a long weekend or reading break. He didn't normally take notice unless they disrupted his class. He sensed tension between Riley and Adam.

But Riley appeared calm – if maybe a little uncomfortable under his teacher's scrutiny. He didn't look like a boy who had punched his best friend. Still, Adam was clearly afraid of him.

"Did you give Mr. Shea that shiner?"

"No sir, I'm no bully."

Mr. Breen narrowed his gaze and pressed his lips together until the boys started to fidget. He shook his head and returned to his desk. Riley might not be lying but he wasn't telling the whole truth. That was fine. He wasn't interested in teen drama and would leave them to sort it out.

Riley had a good head on his shoulders and was one of his better students. The boy was much like his father, who hadn't turned out too badly.

First Contact

Day 113

Ruk pressed the bulbous pads of his two fingers and thumb to a glowing panel next to a closed door. Above the panel was a symbol that Riley had seen before: three intersecting squiggles spewing stars from their tips. It was one of several dozen symbols used on the ship but Riley had discovered the hard way that one symbol could convey a number of different meanings, depending on how it had been scented.

Riley couldn't detect the subtle scents but Lulu had assured him that they were distinct and specific to the individual using the room. Riley had smelled nothing on the door to the rear observation deck on the day that Kar and two male Scouts marked it so that they would not be disturbed. The males had roughed him up and Kar had threatened to

include him in their sexual games if he ever
intruded again.

The panel's glow changed from red to yellow.
Riley followed Ruk into a large room, blank walls
over banks of consoles studded with large levers,
buttons, and blinking lights. As usual, the room
was colder than the hallways. Riley shivered and
pulled his makeshift scarf tighter around his neck,
careful not to bump or touch anything. He'd been
disciplined too many times for casually picking up
tools or opening cupboards to peek inside.

This is a room for observing.

"Like the observation decks? Where are the
windows?"

For observing not what IS but what WAS.

"Right, whatever," Riley muttered under his
breath. Most of Ruk's cryptic comments were
never explained, and asking just got him a nip
from Ruk's teeth or a jab from one of his claw-
tipped fingers.

Riley wandered around the room while Ruk
worked at the controls. All the switches and levers
were chunky, some with holes or straps where
Ruk's many-jointed fingers could slip through for a
tighter grip. For an advanced species, their

awkward hands didn't manipulate objects very well. With only two fingers and a short thumb there was no way for the aliens to achieve any sort of delicate work. It explained their lack of finesse in medicine, and why his fingers had healed crookedly and Lulu's nose didn't sit quite straight on her face.

The room was circular with smooth white walls, unlike the rest of the ship which was painted in a variety of earth tones. Riley pulled his hands into his sleeves to keep them warm and to help him resist the temptation of those many dials and levers. Riley loved electronics and though he'd been gradually given more liberty in the four months he'd been aboard, he still wasn't allowed to touch anything. Ruk had hinted, in his usual gruff manner, that Riley might soon be allowed more privileges and he hoped that would include doing something more than washing his overalls once a week, carrying his own dishes to the chute, and running.

He was going to go crazy if he didn't get to do something soon besides his daily chores. There were no books onboard – not that he'd be able to read their alien script anyway – but also no games or videos, just the endless stars scrolling by outside the observation deck windows.

A loud crackling made him jump, and he turned back to Ruk, who was muttering to himself. All the aliens muttered as they worked, showing intensity or excitement with low squeals and breathy barks.

We have been to your planet before.

"You mean before you kidnapped me and Lulu?" Riley knew that most sarcasm went right over Ruk's head but he couldn't help himself. He also couldn't help his endless questions, risking a jab on the arm or shoulder from Ruk whenever he broached forbidden subjects, but desperate for information on where he was and why he and Lulu had been taken.

Our kind ranges widely to find compatible species.

"I don't like the sound of that," Riley said nervously, thinking of how some of the female Scouts sometimes tried to snuggle close to him in the lounge room, in spite of how badly they treated him the rest of the time.

Metarrans once discovered the means for long life but now our numbers are few. Our females can still produce offspring but many of our males were made sterile by the treatments so now we travel the stars looking to refresh our species.

"Don't look at me," Riley said, crossing his arms stubbornly. "You don't want little Metarran-Rileys running around your ship. Hell, I don't want little Rileys of any kind running around. Not for a long time. Probably never."

Your species has been rejected as too aggressive.

Riley laughed. "Seriously? Your Scouts are way more aggressive than I could ever be. Most of the females are nasty bitches and the males would just as soon punch my face in as look at me."

You are not what they expected to find when we returned to your planet. The Scouts are angry that their parentage is lost in your ancient history.

Riley stared at Ruk's back, wondering if he'd heard correctly. "What do you mean *my* ancient history?"

Ruk adjusted the controls and the crackling sounds intensified as the screen facing Ruk became a starscape. The view jolted and Riley wondered if the ship had hit something. He closed his eyes but felt no movement so he opened them again, and wished he hadn't.

The starry sky now filled the entire room, with white streaks moving past them at a startling speed as they hurtled toward a blue dot that grew larger by the second. Riley grabbed Ruk, certain they were going to be sucked out into space.

A sharp nip on the back of his hand – plus the fact that he wasn't feeling the death pull of an outerspace vacuum – made him let go almost as soon as he'd touched Ruk's arm. Riley lurched to the nearest console and clung desperately as the view began to spiral, taking his stomach along with it.

Ruk whuffed in amusement as he worked the controls, changing the view from a spiral to a steadier streak through the stars.

Close your eyes. Do not vomit on my control panel.

Riley obeyed and closed his eyes. His body stopped swaying as his brain realized that the deck wasn't actually moving. Only his eyes were being fooled.

This is a recording made during our first mission to your planet.

"Oh great, a home movie of my abduction. Do I get popcorn?" He regretted the comment as his stomach rolled again at the mention of food.

Riley had never missed his mother more than he did at this moment. She would have given him an anti-nausea pill long before subjecting him to any sort of travel, knowing how easily he became sick in any moving vehicle where he could see the passing scenery. Movies weren't any better.

You were not abducted. You and the little sister were rescued. It was not a unanimous decision. The Scouts were supposed to observe only, but they are impulsive. The little sister would have died without their action.

These images are of an earlier mission.

Riley opened his eyes a crack, wishing that Ruk had warned him earlier so he could have skipped breakfast. Wisps of clouds streaked by as they plunged toward the surface. Riley's mind – and stomach – still believed that he was falling even though he knew not to trust his eyes. He barely had time to recognize a familiar coastline before they plunged into the foliage of a dense forest. The image was jerked and slammed sideways as they bashed through several trees before coming to a jarring stop.

Riley clutched the console again and squeezed his eyes shut, swallowing convulsively. He slid to the floor and pressed his hands to his temples, trying to stop the spins.

Our shuttle was undamaged so our landing party left to search for any indigenous population.

Riley finally opened his eyes and got to his feet. The view around him had steadied, showing a fine drizzle pattering on deep green leaves.

"So this is my planet?" he asked weakly as he took in the scene. "It looks like they landed in a jungle."

I do not know where we were on your planet but it was your ancient past so the landscape will have changed.

Riley looked at Ruk quizzically. "How far in my ancient past are we talking about here?"

The wall briefly went white again as Ruk touched the controls.

It is much different than when we later found you and the little sister. I saw no technology or manufactured dwellings as in your time.

Ruk pushed another lever and the scene returned, showing the back of an alien trudging through the greenery. Riley heard only grunts, hoots, and the distinctive mutter that he'd been hearing on the ship these past months.

"Why can't I understand what they're saying?"

You were not there to hear. I can translate.

"How? Because you were there to hear?"

Yes, and because they are speaking Metarran.

The rain turned to sleet, interspersed with huge snowflakes that collected on the lens. A furry hand swiped the lens and then curved over the top to shelter it from the thickening snow.

Riley swallowed hard but kept his eyes open even though the image rocked and jolted. "You still haven't said how long ago you made this video."

Time is more flexible on Metarra than it is in your planetary system. Metarra is surrounded by a Deepness that diffuses time as our ships pass through it.

"You mean like how it only took two weeks to get from my planet to yours, but it's gonna take almost a year to get me home?"

The farther we range from Metarra the more the Deepness causes tension to spring us home faster.

"What if your trip out is only like a month or so?"

That is not a long trip and causes no measurable tension. Our return trip would likely take the same time.

Riley stared at Ruk. "That's crazy. So if you went past earth, like maybe twice as far, it might only take you a day to get home?"

Your planet is at the edge of our limits. The Deepness does not allow travel any farther. Its tension eventually affects and slows our progress. When our velocity can no longer resist the tension, we spring home to Metarra.

"Good thing or you'd eventually travel so far that you'd return home before you left," Riley said.

The landing party had come out of the woods into an open space. The scene dipped as the Metarran holding the camera crouched in the tall grass. They all became silent as they watched several animals grazing in the distance.

"Holy crap," Riley whispered in awe. "Are those what I think they are?"

They are impressive beasts.

The scene zoomed in to the largest of the animals. It was enormous, with long dark fur, short legs and two horns on its head: one that curved up from its nose and a shorter horn that sprouted between its eyes. The herd shifted nervously and the Metarrans whisper-muttered with excitement, edging closer with their camera.

"You gotta be kidding me. Those look like woolly rhinos! They went extinct like twenty thousand years ago." Riley stared at the screen, his nausea forgotten for the moment. It was like watching a documentary, except that this didn't look like a staged video and the rhino didn't look like it was just dressed up to look like its prehistoric ancestor.

They were only the first of the aggressive species we met that day.

Riley leaned closer, mesmerized by a scene that no modern human had ever witnessed. "I'm only guessing at twenty thousand years; it could even be thirty! Do you get how long ago that is? This is *way* off course, time-wise."

The largest of the rhinos was now facing the camera and the Metarrans had gone silent again, finally aware of the danger they were in. The huge animal stamped its feet and scraped its thick horn against the ground. It rushed forward several metres, bellowing a challenge. The rest of the herd hung back, keeping their young close.

Many Metarrans got left behind on that day.

Ruk growled as he stared at the screen.

"You're still not getting exactly how long it's been since woolly rhinos lived on my planet. Any Metarrans you left behind are long dead."

At least one survived to breed. The little sister carries Metarran blood.

Riley gaped at Ruk. "Lulu is an alien? Is that why you call her little sister?"

A small part of Lulu comes from one of our landing crew.

"Wait a minute. You came back to rescue an alien that got left behind on my planet twenty thousand years ago? How did you end up finding us?"

The Metarran blood has been much diluted and diffused throughout Lulu's kind. Its signal overwhelmed our initial readings and led us to your time. We could not see past the millions of beings that now carry our blood.

They both turned to the screen again as a new challenge was sounded. The rhinos had all turned to face left, where a small band of hunters had rushed into the clearing. Riley watched, fascinated, as they brandished spears and shouted to hold the rhinos' attention while another group attacked from the right, throwing spears of their own. Three hit their mark, sinking deeply into the side and throat of one of the mid-sized rhinos. It screamed and tossed its head, gouging deeply into the ground with its horn and sending massive clods of earth and snow in the air.

These two-leggeds appeared much larger to me then but I understood later that they were covered in the furs of other beings.

"Oh, man," Riley breathed. "Those are cavemen! Cro-Magnon or something...real prehistoric people!"

At least one is parent to the hybrids.

"Whoa. Did you just say I'm related to the Scouts?"

Ruk nodded. *As is the little sister.*

"Am I related to you?"

No. The Scouts and the little sister share Metarran blood but are born of separate mother races.

"Metarrans came to Earth twenty thousand years ago and bred with wolves and prehistoric humans?" Riley shook his head to clear it. "So Lulu and the Scouts are hybrids but you and me, we're like, pure races?"

I am not so certain of your purity.

On the screen, the injured rhino had stumbled to its knees, hanging its head in pain. It called weakly and fell to one side, snapping the spears against the ground. Thick gouts of blood darkened the snow as the dying animal heaved its last breaths.

The hunters cheered, and another rhino charged toward two of them. They ran for their lives –

straight for the Metarrans. The video caught the hunters' expressions as they spotted the alien beings watching them from the edge of the clearing. They appeared startled by the sight, though more curious than afraid of these furred beings that stood on two legs, as they did.

The rhino didn't follow far and soon turned back to the herd. The animals milled around the massive dead beast, nudging it and snorting nervously. When it didn't rise, they turned and left the clearing in the other direction, their long fur swaying as they ran.

The video didn't follow the woolly rhinos but kept the hunters in sight as they approached. The image trembled, as if the Metarran wearing the camera was barely keeping itself from bolting at the sight of those intense faces. The hunters stopped several metres away, turning at a shout from their comrades, who were swarming the dead rhino. One of them paused to stare intently again at the Metarrans, as if memorizing their features. He then ran to join the others, who were peeling the hide from the dead rhino and carving hunks of steaming meat from its bones.

The video image juddered and went to static before the wall blanked to white. Riley blinked hard. His heart was racing and he was breathing too fast. "That was amazing!" he shouted. Ruk winced and Riley clapped a hand to his mouth. "Sorry," he said silently. "I can't believe what I just saw! Those were, like, prehistoric men hunting woolly rhinos. My father would give anything to see that video, though he probably wouldn't believe it was real." He paced in the small room, running his hands through his short hair.

It is real. The hunters tracked us later and captured most of our crew. I ran for the ship with two others. They were killed with the long sticks and I alone made it. Those who had remained with the ship helped me form a rescue party.

Ruk met Riley's eyes directly.

It took many risings of your sun to find their camp. Only the two females of our crew lived. The others had been thrown into a pit where they were eaten by other predators. We do not know if they were still alive when they were eaten, and we could not tell from the bones how many were there. We saw only three skulls in the pit though four males were missing. We rescued the females but your ancestors had beaten and violated them. They were barely conscious.

Riley sat on the edge of a console. "You keep saying *my ancestors* like they were all bad. Don't blame my whole race for something that happened in our prehistory."

Our people have strived to keep our blood pure but it has not been easy. Our affliction means Metarrans rarely bear pups, but we are adaptable to breeding with many other species. The little sister's blood tells us at least one of our crew was still alive when we left.

"Couldn't you just go back in time again and try again? I mean, before the attack to make sure it didn't happen."

That is what we were doing when we found you and the little sister. The Deepness distortions are unpredictable. Blood calls to blood and is strong enough to overcome the Deepness and grasp a specific point but in your time the Metarran blood is dispersed like a mist throughout your planet. It overshadowed the scent of one Metarran, lost in time.

Riley felt as if a cold hand had squeezed his heart. "Wait a minute. If your rubberband-hyperdrive is so unpredictable, how are you getting me and Lulu back to *our* time? I don't want to end up in some way-distant future."

We follow the scent of the blood you left on the ground. We can bring you back to where we found you. It is still unknown how close to your own time it will be but we are aiming for within a few rotations of your planet.

Riley hoped that Ruk meant they would arrive within a few days of when he and Lulu had been taken – which wouldn't be too bad – but he wasn't sure he trusted that, based on how much time had passed between the Metarrans' first two visits to earth.

Ruk adjusted several dials and headed for the exit, gesturing for Riley to follow. Riley slid off the console and turned back to the view screen.

"Are there any more videos? I don't mean of the capture or rescue or anything like that," he quickly added. "It's just that no one from my time has ever seen anything like this."

There is no more. We did not wish to remain any longer. We released the engines and the Deepness returned us to Metarra.

Neither of the pregnant females survived. Births are such a rare occurrence that we allowed them to reach full term. By then both females were so grossly distended that their bones were breaking.

"Babies broke their mothers' bones?"

The Scouts were much larger than we expected and each had three.

"Lots of human females, um, women have triplets."

Our kind does not have your physical capacity.

Ruk looked up at Riley significantly, and Riley realized that as short as Ruk was, compared to him, the female Metarrans were even smaller.

"So your visit to my planet's caveman-times produced the Scouts for Metarra and modern dogs for Earth. You came back for your lost crewmate and ended up finding Lulu instead, twenty thousand years later." Riley was still struggling with the time difference. "It doesn't explain why you brought the Scouts back to Earth."

It is our custom to bring some hybrids to their ancestral world so that they may choose how they will mature, as full Metarrans or aliens. A few are allowed to remain hybrid but they lack status so most decide against.

Riley nearly bumped into the wall as he glanced sideways at Ruk. "Did you just say they can choose to be one or the other?"

Once hybrids have seen the other world and civilization, some are given the option to choose. Most elect to become full Metarrans and are given a treatment that will change them. That is why we are careful about how we breed as there are consequences to those choices.

"What about Lulu? Are you going to give her a choice too?"

There is so little Metarran blood in the little sister that our Elders have decided to leave her kind as they are. Too many generations have passed for Earth's dogs to be a threat to our species.

"How would you remove the Metarran bits from Kar and the others if they want to be Human?"

We would take blood from you and use its qualities to eradicate all trace of Metarran from their bodies. The process is painful but necessary to keep our bloodlines pure.

"What did they choose?" Riley asked uneasily.

They wish to leave Metarra.

"But earlier you said humans are too aggressive."

Most species are rejected for that reason. We rarely find a species so like our own that we will allow the transformation.

"So you're gonna give them my blood? I'm not sure I like that idea. I mean, that'll make them, like, my relatives or something."

Their choice will not be honoured. They will become fully Metarran.

Riley's Lulu

Lulu slowed her steps as she neared the spot where she and Riley were taken. She sniffed the blood that was now just a brown stain on the grass. Just like at the house, their scents were stronger than they should be, hers still sick and old. The fur on her back rose into a stiff ridge along her spine.

Lulu blood.

A growl rumbled deep in her throat and she scratched at the ground, digging up clods of dirt to bury her scent. She circled the area, sniffing for more, wanting to erase every trace of her old self.

The buzz started again as she finished. She spun in place, straining to reach it, snapping and tugging at her fur, but just couldn't get near the itchy spot. At least it didn't hurt, like the time a wasp got tangled in the silky fur on her belly. The wasp had stung her several times before she'd dropped to the ground and dragged her belly along the sidewalk to crush it.

Lulu whined anxiously as the vibration stopped. She hoped Riley would remember soon why it was there and how to make it stop.

She shook hard to resettle her fur then froze as she heard a sound ahead where the paths crossed. Two voices, nearly the same, whispering and giggling behind a hedge. The two boys that looked and smelled alike.

Lulu remembered how they had laughed as they punched and kicked Riley. She crept closer, keeping to the side of the path. She wanted to sneak up on them and attack before they knew she was even there. Sink her teeth into their skin and make *them* bleed on the grass. Bite the back of their legs so they couldn't run. Claw their faces and chew their fingers bloody.

Lulu paused as they went silent. Had they heard her? She stilled her breath and listened. A third voice cried out and Lulu tensed. She'd heard this voice many times, yelling for Toby. She liked Toby. He smelled good and could run very fast. Lulu crouched and squeezed through a gap in the hedge, emerging several feet away from the trio.

The boys had Tina backed up against the hedge. They were deep enough into the park that no one would see them from the road.

"Leave me alone," Tina said as she moved sideways, the fabric of her jacket making whispery noises as it brushed against stiff holly leaves.

"It's a public park," Jody said.

"Yeah," his brother added. "You never know who you're gonna run into."

"My dad is making lunch for me and I can't be late," Tina said.

"Aw, Daddy's gonna be mad if his little girl is late." Jody grabbed Tina's arm as she tried to move around him. "C'mon, I thought you liked me."

"I think she likes me too," Jerry added and reached for Tina's other arm.

"Let me go!"

Lulu leapt forward and Jerry's grasping fingers closed on air as he was shoved to the ground. She snapped at his face and he wrapped his arms around his head, hollering for his brother.

Girl run.

Lulu turned to Jody, barking savagely. She easily evaded his kicks and grabbed his pant leg but couldn't hold on. The fabric slipped out from between her smooth teeth.

Jody let go of Tina and slapped Lulu's snout. She danced sideways, sneezing at the sharp pain, to attack from another angle.

"That's Riley's dog," Jerry said, picking himself up and rushing to help his brother.

"No way that's the same mutt." Jody feinted left and kicked Lulu in the shoulder as she fell for his ruse and rushed in too close. She yelped but spun around quickly, not wanting to have him behind her.

"We smashed that Fifi to the ground."

No Fifi.

Lulu snarled and snapped her teeth as the brothers tried to grab her. She couldn't keep them both in sight at the same time.

Jody's eyes gleamed. "But I don't mind bashing another Fifi. This one's nasty." He picked up a fallen branch and swung it at Lulu. She ducked and barked shrilly, lunging to snap at his hands.

"You guys leave Lulu alone," Tina shouted.

"I'm sure I said it's not the same dog." Jody turned to his brother. "Didn't I just say it's not the same dog?"

"Yeah, that bitch is gone," Jerry added, moving to his brother's side but far enough apart to force Tina to keep only one of them in her line of sight at a time.

Lulu was uncertain which boy was the biggest threat. She knew that Jerry was the weaker brother, likely to run if she bit him, but Jody might then hurt Tina before she could bite him too.

"If Riley's dog is here, you know he's not far behind," Tina said with more certainty than she felt, as her eyes whipped from one boy to the other.

Riley's Lulu.

Lulu couldn't protect Tina from both boys. She couldn't handle the boys, but she could run. So could Tina. Lulu darted between Jody and Jerry and nipped at Tina's fingers. Tina screeched and jerked her fingers away from Lulu's teeth.

Girl run.

Lulu knew that Tina couldn't hear her but the girl obeyed anyway, slipping to the right and sprinting along the edge of the holly bushes back toward the school. Lulu followed, ready to snap at Tina's heels if she slowed.

The boys were not far behind, shouting insults at Tina and laughing as they followed. They sounded to Lulu like a pack of dogs running down their prey. She barked at Tina to run faster.

Slowly Slowing

Day 176

Lulu nudged Riley's hand, wiggling around so Riley's fingers rested on top of her head. She whined and grumbled until they started to move.

Itchy head.

Riley idly scratched with his eyes closed while he re-counted the marks on the wall he had created in his mind. He'd been trying to keep track of the days so he'd know how long they'd been stuck on the ship but he had nothing to write with and no sharp objects to scratch the wall of his cell.

Every night before falling asleep, Riley closed his eyes and pictured his wall. He imagined himself adding a new mark and counting up the total so he'd at least know what day and month it would be when he woke up. It wasn't easy, knowing that he'd probably missed or forgotten many marks. Ruk said that time passed differently for them but hadn't been able to explain why, though Riley guessed their day was longer than on Earth because he was always exhausted at bedtime, as if he'd stayed up later than usual.

This morning he'd woken with the feeling that he'd fallen asleep before completing his counting exercise. Whenever that happened he simply went through the exercise in the morning, adding the previous day's mark, though he suspected there were many skipped nights he hadn't noticed.

"Doesn't matter which way I count it up," Riley said, finally giving Lulu all of his attention and both hands for a full head scratch. "We've been on this ship for about six months, give-or-take a week or two. That means there's only a few weeks left of school before summer break. Even if we got back tomorrow, I'm so far behind that I'd fail my finals."

Riley miss school.

"Yeah, kind of," Riley answered with a wry grin. "But I won't miss it so much if I have to repeat eleventh grade. Dad won't be very happy about that." His smile faded. "Mom and Dad probably got rid of all my stuff by now and rented out my room to one of his stupid co-op teacher aides."

Riley sighed as he continued to scratch Lulu's face and head. Her fur had completely grown in and now covered the worst of her scars so you couldn't tell they were there unless you felt for them. Her jaw and head had to ache the same way his fingers did but she never complained.

"None of this would have happened if I'd just said no to those guys. Instead, I stole from my dad, messed up my friendship with Adam, and got you hurt."

Lulu not hurt.

"I don't mean now, but before. It was my fault you almost died. You were an old dog and didn't have a chance with those bastards." Riley buried his face in her fur, but Lulu wiggled out and bounced across the room.

Lulu young.

He blew out a frustrated breath. Lulu had never blamed Riley for all the pain she'd endured. He suspected she didn't understand how his stupid actions nearly got her killed, though it might just be that she wasn't buying into his guilt trip.

Riley looked up as the door opened and Ruk entered. He was carrying a tray with their morning meal. He handed one bowl to Riley and set the other on the floor. Lulu wagged her tail in greeting and brushed against Ruk as she hurried to her bowl. Ruk stroked her head in passing and watched them eat.

You are working today with Yerk.

"Oh no," Riley protested. "Not Pee Park again!"

Yerk has been reassigned to a special project. The running track must be scraped and re-moulded. You will pick up the scrapings.

"That track is like a quarter mile long. It'll take us forever."

It cannot. Metarrans will not like to miss their daily run so you must work quickly.

Riley finished his breakfast, grumbling as he tilted his bowl for the last mushy bits. "I'm going to go crazy. There's nothing to do here but run and work."

Play fetch.

Lulu wagged her tail hopefully.

Yes, fix the track and you can play fetch, or race-tag.

127

"The Scouts cheat at race-tag and I always come out with bruises. They change rules randomly and get mad if I happen to win." Riley frowned when Ruk snorted in amusement.

They claim the same of you.

"They'll be glad when I'm off this ship. Are you sure you're going the right way? Are we even close to getting me and Lulu home?"

We are slowly slowing.

"Wait a minute," Riley said, leaning forward and setting his bowl by the door. "You've been saying *approaching soon* for weeks. How long is *slowly slowing* going to take?"

Ruk blinked at Riley and shook his head.

"Forget I asked." Riley sighed and settled back, motioning for Lulu to jump up. "Even if I could get a straight answer out of you, it probably wouldn't make sense."

Lulu turned in place a couple of times before settling her warm bulk against Riley's side. She wagged her tail and whuffed at Ruk.

Kar say stupid.

"Putt-Putt is just being mean and you don't have to listen." Riley scratched her head, focusing on the lumpy tissue that was always itchy.

The Scouts are on edge because we are slowing. The trip is nearly at its end. Their lives will change when they return to Metarra.

"So that gives them the right to be jerks? Kar goes out of her way to abuse Lulu."

The Scouts have discovered they will not be allowed to make the change to Human. They are very angry. Do not provoke them unnecessarily. We believe it is their Human blood which makes them lash out.

"I guess I'd be mad too if I wasn't allowed to make my own choices." Riley looked pointedly at Ruk, who ignored the jab.

One of your kind's most dangerous traits is your tendency to make choices for your own individual good.

"What's wrong with making choices that are right for me?"

It is why your planet is overpopulated and stripped of resources. We were once in danger of reaching the same limits but found a way to slow our excessive population growth by removing our personal choice.

"What do you mean?"

We took away choices and selectively bred to veer toward our ancestors' tendencies, disallowing most pairings so that we would not overburden Metarra. The scientific advances that extended our lives satisfied those who were angry at not being allowed to breed.

"Yeah, and it backfired on you." Riley crossed his arms. "You tried to slow down population growth with science and messed it up. How many kids are born on Metarra these days?"

The Scouts are the first hybrids in many generations who survived birth and there had not been any pure Metarrans for a generation before that.

Riley gazed at Ruk pensively. He'd guessed Ruk was old because of the white fur that salted his muzzle but it sounded like this had happened a long time ago. "Were you one of the last ones born?"

Ruk shook his head. *I was already old when I began the treatments. I have now lived many of your Human generations.*

"If the Scouts might live to be hundreds of years old it's not so surprising they still act like annoying teenagers."

They are not adolescents. Metarrans mature at forty years and the scouts are nearly twice that. Their behaviour is unpredictable and at times destructive and angry.

"More like forty going on fourteen," Riley said with a smirk. "They probably challenge you all the time and then come running for attention whenever they're scared. You wonder if they'll ever grow up when they're constantly fighting and acting like jerks." He pushed both his hands into Lulu's fur to warm his fingers. She yawned and closed her eyes.

Our science will make them more Metarran but it cannot happen until they mature and our fear is that they may become more aggressive before that time. They are not like most hybrids. We have not ever met beings like you.

"I know plenty of kids at my school who are jerks but will probably grow out of it, but there are other kids who have aggro parents and don't know any better."

The scouts are difficult individuals but I promised their mothers I would care for them.

"No one promised *my* mother they'd care for *me*."

Ruk looked at Riley for a long moment before nodding his head.

I will be more patient with them and with you.

Lulu yawned again and shook herself. She looked up at Riley.

Lulu run.

"Sure. Do you want to chase too?"

Yes chase.

Lulu barked excitedly while Riley dug behind the mattress for the knotted fabric ball he'd made for her. It didn't throw far, but there wasn't really anywhere far to throw on the ship except along the running track.

Ruk watched from the door with a pensive expression.

Are all Human adolescents like you?

"I'm pretty typical but like I said, not all humans are aggressive." He found the ball and tossed it to Lulu, who caught it in mid-air.

Do not play long. There is another task for you.

"Oh great, more chores," Riley said, rolling his eyes. "Any more fun than picking up scraps behind Yerk?"

We are receiving signals from your planet. We are approaching where we found you but must narrow the when. There is much screeching and static in the transmissions. You will translate any clear signals and work to narrow our trajectory.

Riley's mouth dropped open. "You're getting s-signals f-from Earth?" He stared at Ruk. "You never told me you had a radio I could use. I could have sent a signal home months ago!"

We were not receiving signals before now so there was no reason for you to monitor the communication console.

"Can I go listen now?" He almost tripped over Lulu, who was prancing around him in circles.

Throw ball.

Ruk palmed open the door and Lulu rushed out with her cloth ball. She dropped it and ran partway down the hall, turning to bounce in place.

The ball was already soggy. Riley sent it sailing over Lulu's head but she leapt up and easily caught it before racing away. Riley knew she would wait for him outside the track entrance.

"Maybe the radio will pick up some music, though I'll be happy to hear even the stupidest commercials." He grinned at Ruk, who shook his head.

This is not a game for your amusement. You will begin your new task after you have assisted Yerk. I suspect the track will gain its new surface quickly.

Riley felt a stab of impatience but knew Ruk was right. The running track would get done in record time if it meant getting to use a radio. He ran after Lulu, wondering if Ruk understood how much this meant to him, and if he'd known that Riley was bored out of his mind and afraid they'd never make it home.

Dumb Puppies

Riley wove through the crowd, trying to keep Adam in sight. All around him kids were joking and laughing, doing all the things he remembered doing the last time he'd been hanging around the school halls. Some of the guys called out to him and he waved but kept moving. Nothing had changed for them and this was just another ordinary day, just like with his parents.

Riley felt like he'd moved away and was back for a visit. It was surreal, as if he'd missed an entire school year. Everything was familiar and strange at the same time. No wonder he couldn't remember his locker combination.

He passed a huddle of girls who stared silently as he approached and burst into giggles after he passed. His face burned as he glanced back at them. They had never paid attention to him before today and he frowned in confusion. He wondered if his dad's clothes were even dorkier than he'd thought. He'd been wearing Metarran coveralls for so long that it felt weird to be in jeans.

Riley lost sight of Adam as he burst out the front doors into the school yard. He craned his neck, scanning past the knots of teens, finally spotting Adam running for the railway tracks.

Riley hurried across the road, keeping his head down when he saw Matt talking to some girls. He took a shortcut between two houses, jumping over a row of jammed-together recycling bins that clogged the alleyway and scaring a cat that was napping on a discarded sofa. He followed the garbage-strewn fence that ran the length of the housing project and saw Adam heading for the middle of town.

It felt good to run with the wind in his face after being confined to the ship's running track for so long. Riley lengthened his stride and easily closed the gap. "Adam, wait up," he shouted. "I just want to talk."

Adam looked over his shoulder and tripped, flailing his arms for balance. He stumbled to a stop and bent over, bracing his hands on his knees as he panted for breath. He eyed Riley warily. They'd been friends forever and hung out nearly every day after school, goofing around, playing video games or watching movies.

And last night he'd crushed his best friend's hand under his boot heel.

"You're not even…breathing…hard," Adam gasped. "What the hell happened to you?" He straightened and took a step back to put more distance between them.

"I got shit-kicked," Riley answered. "Don't tell me you've already forgotten. I got a matching shiner at the same party." He leaned in so Adam could see that his eye had long healed.

"I went back for you later, after those guys ditched me." Adam took a quick step back to put more space between them.

"Lulu and I weren't going to hang around so you could sneak back for second helpings."

Adam pointed at Riley's hand. "Looks like it didn't get broken after all. I guess the ground was pretty soft and cushioned your hand. That's a relief!" Adam's weak grin faded as Riley brought both hands up and closed the right into a tight fist. The left stopped halfway, making a white-knuckled claw with a pinkie that bent to the side.

"Oh yes, it was broken. We both know that."

"Broken bones can't heal overnight so it must just be sprained." Adam couldn't meet Riley's piercing glare and turned away to stare up the track. He put a few more steps between them before facing Riley again.

"You know I didn't mean to do it, right?" His voice shook and he felt his throat tighten. "I'm so sorry but those guys forced me to...to..." Adam wiped tears with his sleeve. He took a few calming breaths and tried to look anywhere but at his best friend. "You just look so different."

"I look different? You mean not bloody? It really is just the next day for you, isn't it?"

"Of course it's the next day," Adam cried. "What are you talking about? Those guys beat the crap out of you. You should be a mess!" He flinched as Riley raised his eyebrows. "They beat me too, you know," Adam finished miserably.

Riley watched the younger boy working out the impossible in his mind. He reminded himself that he'd forgiven Adam months ago. "I know. I've thought about that a lot lately."

"What do you mean *lately*? It happened yesterday!"

Riley stepped closer to Adam. "How tall was I the last time you saw me?"

Adam eyed him up and down, noting that Riley was taller, and broader at the shoulders than he remembered.

"Do you get it yet?" Riley smirked at Adam's dumfounded look. "Yesterday I had three broken fingers and a couple of cracked knuckles." He flexed his fingers again. "As you can see, they're fixed but they don't work so well anymore. The doc who set the bones wasn't used to *human* fingers."

"That's crazy talk," Adam said nervously. "You can't heal up like this in only one day."

"But you can do a lot of healing in 241 days." Riley kicked at the gravel. "I feel so ripped off. It should be July, not November. I was hoping for sunshine after being cooped up so long."

"That's impossible. I just saw you."

"And then you ran off. We weren't there when you came back. You should have hung around for a while. We weren't gone long."

Adam knew the only way Riley could have healed so thoroughly was with time, like maybe 241 days' worth. He shifted his feet nervously. "So that light wasn't the police?"

"Not even close." Riley grinned. "We got abducted by aliens. We traveled through outer space on an alien ship for eight months while only an hour passed for everyone else."

"That's impossible," Adam repeated. "You can do better than that." He gave a half-hearted eye roll for effect but couldn't ignore the changes in Riley. Anyone could fake a deeper voice, but Riley was bigger and his face was older too.

"This didn't just grow overnight, you know." Riley stroked the brown fuzz above his upper lip.

"You call that a mustache?" Adam asked, smiling weakly. "Wait a minute! If your crazy story is true, that means you're, like, already sixteen."

"Coming up on seventeen, sort of, but don't tell my Mom. She'll want Dad to talk to me about all the changes I should expect as I come into my manhood."

They both laughed, though Adam wasn't convinced that his beating hadn't damaged his brain so that he was hallucinating.

The wind was chilly and Adam turned up his collar. "What was it like?" he asked, feeling a little crazy for even asking. He jammed his hands in his pockets, wishing he had worn a scarf.

"I had a lot of time to think," Riley replied. "There wasn't much else to do."

Adam raised a skeptical eyebrow. "You want me to believe you've been on a spaceship – with aliens – but you were bored?"

"Lulu and I weren't really in any shape to do much of anything at first, and the aliens didn't like us much so we were usually left on our own later."

Where Riley?

"That's Lulu," Riley said, turning to face back the way they'd come.

"What? I don't hear Lulu." Adam felt a stab of fear as he remembered the last time he'd seen Lulu, lying on the ground and bleeding from her mouth and nose.

"You won't." He put two fingers in his mouth for a piercing whistle.

Boys chase Lulu.

"Sounds like trouble. Someone's chasing her. Probably your new friends."

"Not *my* friends," Adam said. "Besides, I saw what Lulu looked like after Matt kicked her. No way is she running today."

"She's alive and well, and pissed at you." Riley looked hard at Adam. "You'd better be standing on our side when she gets here."

"Doesn't matter which side I'm on now," Adam said miserably, meeting Riley's gaze. "Lulu's going to chew my face off."

"Decide. Are you one of the bad guys?" Riley crossed his arms and waited.

See Riley.

Riley spotted Lulu and Tina charging up the gravel bank side-by-side, with two larger figures closing in on them. The expression on Lulu's face darkened when she recognized Adam. Riley stepped in front of him barely in time to intercept Lulu, who dove for Adam's throat.

"No, Lulu!"

Bite Adam.

Tina ran past, circling the scuffling trio. Jody and Jerry skidded to a stop, hanging back as they took in the scene. Tina crouched behind Adam and caught her breath, keeping one eye on Lulu's snapping teeth and the other on the thick branch that Jerry was carrying. He snapped off the smaller twigs from his makeshift club and swung it over his head, grinning and jostling his brother.

"Lulu, don't do this," Riley pleaded, shoving the dog away from Adam. She stumbled and fell, churning up the gravel as she scrabbled to her feet and tried to skirt around Riley.

Say Adam bully.

"Lulu says you're a bully." Riley put a restraining hand on Lulu's head. She snorted and shook him off but stayed where she was. She stared hard at Adam, her lip curled in a snarl.

Adam stared back in amazement. Lulu was young and strong, with glossy fur and clear eyes. But she was an old dog the last time Adam saw her, limping and nearly blind. How could she be young again?

"I would never hurt you, Lulu," Adam whispered.

"But you did hurt me." Riley held up his left hand. "That's why she's so mad."

"She didn't see that happen," Adam protested, knowing that Lulu had not moved again after she'd crumpled to the ground.

"Lulu saw how messed up I was when she woke up. I had to tell her everything that happened after Matt put her in that coma."

"What coma?" Tina asked. She had inched forward so she was standing just behind Adam. "And what happened to you?" She blushed but continued to stare at him, wide-eyed.

"It's a long story," Riley answered. He held her gaze for a moment, wondering why he'd never noticed her eyes were the same blue as the sky. He grinned shyly and turned back to Adam. "Tell Lulu you're sorry."

"What are you talking about?" Adam asked, his voice cracking with fear. "How is she even walking? She was bleeding and all smashed up."

"Tell Lulu that you're sorry you hurt me."

"Sorry? Of course I'm sorry!"

Lulu yell.

Lulu pushed past Riley and barked ferociously at Adam, then poked him hard in the stomach. Adam grunted in pain and dropped to his knees. Lulu grabbed the sleeve of his jacket and shook him hard.

Give special food.

"What for?"

Lulu yell Adam.

"No. You heard him. He said he was sorry."

Say Adam bad.

"Yeah, Lulu, he knows he was bad. Now let him go."

Without warning, Jerry swung at Lulu. She yelped as the club connected with her rump and she spun around to snarl at him. Riley stepped to her side and Jerry faltered, eyeing Riley suspiciously.

"You boys need to stop bashing on my dog." Riley side-stepped the branch aimed at his face and punched Jerry in the shoulder, forcing him to drop it. Jerry cursed and dove for it but Riley kicked it out of his reach.

Jody was staring hard at Riley. "Who fixed your face? Or didn't we leave you enough souvenirs?"

"Same way I managed to grow two inches and gain about twenty pounds, moron. Time fixes everything – eventually."

Riley remember!

"Yeah, Lulu, I remember all of it now." Riley ruffled Lulu's ears as she panted happily up at him. "We're done here," he continued quietly, realizing he wasn't afraid of Jody and Jerry, not even a little. "You guys are going to leave us alone. All of us," he said, gesturing behind him where Tina and Adam huddled together. "It was stupid of me to steal my father's test papers for you idiots." He looked at Adam and smiled apologetically. "Even stupider of me to fill it in with wrong answers. You were right, Adam. I should have said no the first time."

"Are you lovebirds finished making up yet?" Jerry asked, stepping forward. He stopped at Lulu's warning bark. "And where the fuck did you get another stupid Fifi so fast?"

"Same dog, moron," Riley said mildly.

Lulu snarled and leaped for Jerry. Riley grabbed her by the collar before she could do more than snap at his face.

Jerry stumbled back from the furious dog and pointed at Adam. "Come on," he said. "Let's finish what we started last night. You'll make us three against one. The chick and Fifi don't count."

Adam stepped up to stand next to Riley and Tina joined him. He glanced at Lulu but averted his gaze when she growled softly.

Bad Adam.

Riley let go of Lulu's collar. "You guys are outnumbered," Riley said to the twins. "Adam isn't your friend. He only did what you told him to because he was terrified of being beaten. But then you beat him anyway." Riley stepped forward and grabbed Jody by the front of his jacket, jerking him off balance. He cupped his left hand around the back of Jody's neck and turned him to face the others.

Jerry moved to help his brother but Lulu lunged at him, snapping at his face. He cursed in panic and ran back toward the school, with Lulu hot on his heels.

Jody tried to pull away from Riley. "Let me go," he spat, kicking at Riley's shins.

"Not quite yet." Riley forced him toward Tina and Adam. "Apologize to Tina," he said and released

Jody, who tripped and stumbled into her. She pushed him away and slapped his face loudly. Jody was too startled to react before Tina slapped his other cheek. Tears sprung to his eyes and he took a step back when Adam's hands closed into fists.

"That's enough," Riley said. "No one needs to beat on anyone else today." He stared at Adam until the younger boy nodded, then he turned back to Jody. "Get the hell out of here. If I ever catch you bothering any of my friends again, I'll see you get what you deserve."

"That bitch better not bite my brother," Jody snarled, wiping his eyes on his sleeve. He backed away, stumbling in the shifting gravel.

Riley peered into the distance. "Then you'd better hurry before Lulu mangles him too much. She may be the same dog, but she's not the same *kind* of dog anymore."

Good Dog

Day 241

The deck rumbled under Riley's feet for the third time since breakfast. It pressed against his boot soles incrementally as the ship slowed. Riley swallowed hard against nausea as his stomach rolled again. They had been *slowly slowing* for months, as increased distance from Metarra stretched the space that Ruk called the Deepness, but in the last couple of days the engines had been reversing in bursts to slow them even more. According to Ruk, once they fully stopped in Earth's orbit they would only have a limited time before tension forced them to release and they boomeranged home.

Riley wiggled around in his seat, trying to find a comfortable spot. The chair was contoured for a Metarran body, angled forward to accommodate a crouched posture with a hole at the back for a tail.

To Riley it felt more like perching than sitting, and he couldn't manage more than a couple of hours at a time, which still left him with an aching back and leg cramps.

The first two fingers of each hand were jammed deeply into the embedded controls in the chair's console arms. Suction held them in the channels which, luckily for Riley, were soft-sided and accommodated his crooked left fingers. He'd tried to work the radio without actually sitting in the chair, but the angle and size of the controls made it impossible.

He dug deeper, trying to ignore the sticky moisture that constantly seeped into the angled holes. It was supposed to make him more receptive to incoming signals so he could follow them, or so Ruk said.

Riley hated this stupid ship. Every knob or handle was made to be manipulated with two fingers and a thumb, extra-long. The aliens' fingers also bent in directions that Riley's fingers didn't, so many of their tools were impossible for him to use.

His right hand controlled the tuning and his left worked volume. The controls lagged in response to pressure from Riley's weaker – and shorter – fingers. He couldn't quite reach the bottom of the holes to make fine adjustments so tuning to faint signals was difficult and some days took more patience than Riley had ever imagined he had.

The back of the seat curved over into a hood that ended below his ears, with speakers on either side. It forced his head forward and down so he had to stare at his knees while he listened.

Riley ducked his head at a loud burst of static and winced at the ache in his left hand as he increased pressure to lower the volume, trying to keep his right hand steady so he didn't lose the signal. It took constant, even pressure to keep the tuner in one spot. He raised his head back into the hood so he could listen closely while his tuner hand altered pressure back and forth to explore the static.

A thin squeal and then a voice he'd heard a dozen times in the last week came through. A woman shouted in a language Riley couldn't understand while tinny music played in the background. The signal was clearer than ever, and Riley closed his eyes while he listened to one of only six separate signals he'd managed to find. Ruk could locate dozens more, but he had to sit in the chair to do it and then Riley couldn't hear the faint signals through the hood. It was frustrating and almost not worth the time spent contorted in that tiny space, but he listened daily, hoping to hear something familiar.

Riley twitched when he heard a soft grunt behind him, and the signal slid back into static. He swore under his breath and pulled his fingers out of the console, which released them with a disgusting viscous slurp. He wiped them on his pant legs, not looking at the yellow glop. It turned his stomach at the best of times. Today he was already so queasy that he could smell it, though he knew the substance was odourless.

We have arrived at your world.

Riley hurled himself out of the chair, banging his head on the hood and his hip on the console. He stumbled and faced Ruk, who was standing at the entrance to the radio room with a look of amusement on his furry face.

"Why didn't you tell me we were almost there? A little notice would have been nice so I could at least have a shower before going home."

We could not know we had arrived until we arrived.

"That's Ruk-logic for you," Riley said. His mouth dropped open in surprise when he recognized what Ruk was carrying. "Is that my backpack?"

You must leave behind all you wear. Your garments are inside.

Riley stripped off the one-piece coverall and soft booties that he'd worn daily for months and happily pulled on his old clothes. They were tight and he barely managed to button his jeans and stuff his feet into his boots. Everything smelled musty but he couldn't help grinning at the sight and feel of his own clothes. He pulled on his jacket and jammed his arms through the backpack's straps.

"Are we at least close to my house? What day is it? I'm sure I missed counting a few days, if not a couple of weeks, though it won't matter to my parents if I've been gone almost a year," he finished glumly.

He started down the hall toward his room but Ruk pulled on his arm.

You must go now.

"I'm not leaving without Lulu," Riley said. He tried to yank his arm back but Ruk tightened his grip and growled. His fur was bristling, making him look larger than he was.

Lulu is already in the transport room. There is no time to waste.

Riley cast a worried glance at Ruk, who avoided looking directly at him as he hurried down the hall.

"No need to drag me. You do remember this is the day I've been waiting for," Riley said with a nervous laugh. They passed through a door into a part of the ship that he hadn't ever been allowed in. They hurried down several identical hallways before Ruk finally stopped and looked at Riley.

The hybrids are on edge and may cause trouble.

"What kind of trouble?"

They have discovered that Lulu and her kind will not be forced to make the change and will be left as they are.

"So what?" Riley was uneasy. He could hear growling and shouting on the other side of the door, and some of the voices were starting to worm their way into his thoughts.

It is important that you do as I say after we enter the room. Many things may happen that you must allow.

Ruk pulled a small sack from a belt pouch and thrust it at Riley, who shoved it into his pants pocket.

It is the special food and will keep your link with Lulu for some time. Use it sparingly and it will last longer, though you will need to remain close to speak.

Ruk pressed his long fingers to a light pad on the wall. The door slid open and Riley was engulfed in a roar of too many voices, assaulting his mind and his ears. The room was too warm and smelled musky, a scent that Riley associated with anger and aggression among the Scouts, all six of whom had come to see him and Lulu off.

He'd never been to this room and scanned the huge space for Lulu. He heard her a second before she rushed him and pressed against his legs.

Putt-Putt chase Lulu.

The room had gone quiet at Riley's entrance and every eye was turned to him and Lulu. He laid a hand on her trembling head. "Don't worry, we're going home and you won't have to ever see her again." He turned to Ruk. "How close are we?"

Ruk nodded to the Alpha who was sitting at a console and one of the walls dissolved to show a blue and green planet, bright against a black starry night. Riley stumbled into the room to stand in front of the screen, where the Scouts were jostling each other and growling. Lulu stayed glued against Riley, whining nervously.

"That's amazing," he whispered. "Just like one of those images from the space station." He called to Ruk, who had moved to a recessed alcove and was talking to Mirt and two other Alphas. "What's the date?"

You know we do not count time as you do. Your timepiece is also in your pack. It will tell you the when of your arrival.

Kar sidled closer and squatted to Lulu's eye level.

I have a gift for you.

No gift.

You have no choice, little sister.

Kar grabbed Lulu's collar and, before Riley could react, Pru jabbed something into Lulu's lower back. There was a snap and hiss. Lulu yelped and shook her head fiercely to dislodge Kar, who laughed and released her, jumping away to avoid Lulu's teeth.

Now we can find you again.

"What did you do to her?" Riley asked, running his hands over Lulu's back. There was blood on her fur and a bump under her skin.

It is only a beacon and will not harm the little sister.

Ruk and Mirt had left the alcove and were huddled with several Alphas. Every being in the room was talking, most of them out loud, and Riley could hardly hear himself think. Mirt nodded and another Alpha barked out a command.

Riley and Lulu were pushed into the empty alcove. It was dim inside, with not a lot of room to spare. The transparent walls were thick and silenced the inner babble but showed the Scouts pressing close. He grabbed Lulu before she could lunge at Kar.

"Leave her alone, Lulu," he begged. "We're out of here any minute now and you won't ever have to see Putt-Putt again."

Yes, our time here is short. The Deepness will soon recall the ship but we will return later to live on your planet. Metarra rejects us as we are, but your kind is diverse and will accept us.

"Are you kidding?" Riley gaped at Kar. "You think Metarran hybrids could live on my planet? You can't come to Earth looking like that, even with your caveman DNA. You don't look anything like us."

We are half-Human and will learn to fit into your society. Human blood has made Scouts fully bipedal, as you are. Our prehistory was four-legged but Scouts have evolved beyond Metarrans, who still run on all fours, like our ancestors.

"You're still aliens. You'll be put in cages and scientists will experiment on you. They'll never let you out."

You will tell them we treated you well and they will do the same for us.

"They won't believe that," Riley said desperately, holding tightly to Lulu. "Look, if my people get even a hint that aliens came to our planet – and more than once – they'll seriously freak out."

Ruk and Mirt pushed past Kar and squeezed into the alcove. Lulu shook her head and Riley let go of her collar so she could snuffle Ruk's outstretched fingers.

"Ruk, tell them. You know Humans are not as nice as Metarrans. They'll question the Scouts and then come looking for you. Your elders won't like that."

The Deepness is strong at this distance and the ship cannot hold its tension for long. You must go.

Ruk held Riley's gaze. The muscles on his snout twitched, as if he had more to say.

Mirt pulled out another tool like the one Kar had used on Lulu and aimed it at Riley's head. Lulu growled and Riley went still, all his attention focused on Mirt.

"If I have to get a beacon too I'd rather not have it embedded in my head," he said, careful not to move anything but his eyes.

It is not a beacon.

Ruk took the tool from Mirt, who left the alcove with a grunt. Ruk pressed the tip against Riley's neck and Riley gasped as he felt a sharp pinch.

Now you will forget.

"I'll never forget you, buddy," he said and pressed a hand to his neck. He blinked a few times, feeling a strange tingle spreading from his neck up into his head.

You will forget.

"And now you're repeating yourself." Riley's voice sounded strange to him, too loud and drawn-out. The tingle grew to a throbbing pressure behind his eyes. He steadied himself with a hand on Lulu's head. "Your beacon packs a punch."

It is not a beacon but a memory wipe.

Ruk stepped around to face them. He reached out and hugged Riley, setting off howls of protest outside the alcove. Riley resisted but Ruk held him tightly, pressing his muzzle against the side of Riley's face.

You must remove Lulu's beacon. The hybrids must not be allowed a link to this planet. I have manipulated the ship's drive and our return trajectory will take us far beyond Metarra.

Riley pulled back and looked at him with half-lidded eyes. "Don't worry, fuzz-face," he said, starting to sway. "No one's gonna take over the world, not as long as I can help it." He reached out and ruffled the fur on Ruk's head, something he had never dared.

Ruk crouched and reached for Lulu, scratching her ears. She whined and licked his face.

Riley will need your help after he forgets.

"My head really hurts. What the hell happened, Lulu?" Riley pulled her to him, eyeing the others warily. He frowned and shook his head to clear it.

Lulu and Riley go home.

Kar stepped away from the others and leaned in to Lulu.

We will see you soon, little sister.

Ruk shoved her away and stood between the Scouts and the alcove.

Lulu is not your little sister. She is a good dog.

The door slid shut. The walls shifted to opaque. Riley and Lulu were alone in the silence and darkness.

Go home.

The space around them filled with a blast of brilliant light. A loud, throbbing hum dropped Riley to his knees and he wrapped his arms around his aching head, confused and terrified. He whimpered and thought he heard Lulu barking.

Then the floor disappeared from under his feet.

Lulu Bark

They were hidden from sight, deep enough into the forest to avoid most of the popular trails. It was late afternoon and the sun provided barely enough light to see clearly, its winter rays split into jagged streaks by the bare branches overhead.

Riley had stopped home long enough after school for a snack and to grab the first aid kit from the camping gear stored in the basement. He left a note saying he wouldn't be late and he and Lulu had sped through the woods, following a path they hadn't run for years.

They had about an hour before dark, just enough time to get it done. Riley took a deep breath and pressed the tip of his mother's sharpest paring knife against Lulu's skin. He'd doused the knife with alcohol to sterilize it and wore latex gloves that he'd found in the first aid kit.

Lulu whined but held steady as the blade pricked her flesh and bright red blood seeped into her fur. The knife felt awkward in his right hand but at least he could hold it tightly and more steadily than his weaker left.

"Are you sure about this?" he asked, blotting the blood with a handful of gauze. He'd trimmed away some of the fur around the swollen red bump under Lulu's skin.

Out now.

"I don't want to hurt you any more than I have to," he said. "We could still take you to the vet and at least get it done right, with anesthetic so it wouldn't hurt." He was only half serious, since he had no idea how he'd explain that aliens had implanted a homing beacon in his dog.

Not hurt.

Lulu licked his hand and laid her head on her paws, holding as still as possible when Riley sliced deeper. She whined again when the knife scraped against a hard surface.

"Sorry," Riley said through chattering teeth. The temperature was dropping but he was sweating. He could hardly stand to be doing this, cutting into Lulu with a knife. He wiped his sleeve across his face to clear his eyes and picked up the tweezers. They were easier for his left hand to manage since he only needed his thumb and index finger for pinching.

Riley kept the tip of the blade steady against the beacon and slid the tweezers next to it. He could barely see what he was doing because of the blood but tried to move the tools as little as possible. Lulu shivered as the tweezers gripped the beacon and he eased it from her flesh.

"I got it," Riley said, his voice cracking. He dropped a tiny sliver onto a square of gauze and covered it with another to soak up the blood. It was an inch long and as slim as a toothpick.

Lulu moved and fresh blood welled from the wound.

Smash beacon.

"Hold still. Let me bandage you first." He had to keep Lulu away from the tiny sliver. She'd try to bite it and might swallow it by accident. Ruk said the beacon had to be destroyed and Riley wasn't going to let it out of his sight until he did just that.

Riley pressed a wad of gauze against Lulu's skin to stop the bleeding. When it slowed, he added another layer and taped it to her fur. The bandage was sloppy and would fall off soon, but he didn't want to cut any more fur off or his parents would notice.

Lulu bounded to her feet and twisted awkwardly to sniff the bandage near her tail. She flicked her tongue but barely reached the edge of the tape.

Still itchy.

"Good thing you can't scratch it or you'd have to wear the cone." Riley used more gauze to wipe Lulu's blood from the knife and tweezers, and grinned at Lulu's sneer of disdain. She'd only ever worn the plastic cone once, after she'd sliced her paw on some glass and the wound became infected because she wouldn't stop licking it. When his dad decided her paw was healed enough to take the cone off, Lulu had snatched it up and run for the basement. By the time Riley caught up, she'd chewed enough holes in the plastic to render it useless.

He tossed the bloody gauze into a plastic bag and peeled off his gloves, adding them to the bag, which he tied shut and shoved into a side pocket of his backpack. The knife and tweezers went into the first aid kit. He grabbed Lulu's chin and turned her head to get her full attention.

"It has to stay clean. We can't take the chance it'll get infected. And don't let Dad see it or he'll think you got into a fight with a raccoon again." Riley knew she got the message when her eyes narrowed. Lulu thought of raccoons as fat cats with an attitude problem, but it was the most plausible story if his dad saw the wound.

Smash now.

"All right, I'll need a rock," Riley said and set the beacon on a flat spot. Lulu raced off, wagging her tail. The beacon skittered sideways with a faint buzz just as Lulu dropped a fist-sized rock at Riley's feet.

He wondered what sort of signal it was sending. Could the Scouts really find them again just by following this tiny sliver? Lulu barked sharply and Riley finally hit it with the rock, stilling its buzz. He bashed it repeatedly until nothing was left but a few sprinkles of metal.

"That's as smashed as it's going to get." He threw the rock aside and swept the beacon's remains to the ground with the side of his hand. Lulu scratched at the dirt vigorously, dispersing the metallic bits in a wide area.

"You can relax now. There's no way they can track you without the beacon." Riley checked her bandage. It was holding so far. "It might hurt for a while."

No hurt.

They slumped together on the yellowed grass, enjoying the last weak rays of the setting sun on their faces. Lulu laid her head on Riley's knee for an ear scratch. They hadn't come this far into the woods since Lulu's arthritic hips had stiffened and she couldn't manage the climb from the main road up through the woods.

"What happens when I can't hear you in my head anymore?"

Lulu loud.

"Sure, for a while anyway, but that won't work once the special food is out of our systems. We don't know how long we have."

Lulu bark.

He threw her an admiring glance. "That makes the most sense. You understand a lot of the words I use so I should try to understand what you're always barking about.

Riley got to his feet. "Okay, so if you're hungry, bark once." Lulu barked and pranced when Riley clapped in praise. "Now, bark twice like you need to go out."

Lulu barked and waited but Riley only frowned so she barked again and poked his leg with her snout.

"We might have a problem," he said and sat again.

Say bark.

"Yeah, but I said bark twice and you only barked once." He rested his elbows on his knees. "You can't count any better than you can tell time."

Bark hungry.

Lulu barked once.

Bark pee.

She barked again.

"They sound exactly the same."

Riley listen.

Lulu barked once, paused, and barked again.

"The second bark was higher pitched?"

Riley smart.

Riley got his face licked. "I *thought* I was," he said with a sigh.

Lulu talk.

"Yeah, I get it. I'm the one who has to figure out what you're saying. We'll have to work fast, before our ESP powers run out."

Riley listen.

"Ruk said you might live as long as I will, so it's worth learning as much as I can while I can still hear you," he said, scratching behind her ears. "It'll be more interesting than any project I'll ever do in school."

Lulu tensed and cocked her ears forward, staring intently over his shoulder. A second later, Riley heard rustling near the road.

"Maybe that's Adam," he said, standing and checking that he'd put everything away. Adam was already freaked out; he didn't need to catch Riley with a bloody knife.

Adam not pack.

"Yes he is," Riley corrected. "Adam is my friend and he only did what Matt told him to so they'd stop hurting him."

Matt hurt Adam.

"Exactly. A mean alpha is going to have a mean pack." Lulu growled softly but Riley quieted her with a head shake. "We'll be a good pack so Adam will be good too."

A dog came bursting out of the bushes into the meadow and ran up to Lulu. They touched noses and circled to sniff under each other's tail, wagging happily.

Smell good.

"Too much information, thanks," Riley said with a laugh.

Tina smell good?

Riley felt himself blush. "Shut up!" He thumped her side. "Go run."

Lulu raced away in pursuit of her new friend. Riley lost sight of them but could hear the dogs crashing through the dry brush. The sun was gone and shadows were thickening. A thin mist hovered above the dried grass.

Riley tipped his head back and breathed deeply. The cool breeze was fresh, not like the stale air in the ship. Stars were appearing across the darkening sky. He picked out Orion – the only constellation he knew – and thought it might be cool to learn about the other stars he could see, now that he'd been flying among them. His dad would be pleased at his new interest in astronomy; maybe enough to spring for a telescope.

Riley could hardly believe that only a day had passed since he and Lulu were on an alien space ship. He'd gotten used to it, especially when he'd believed they'd never get home, but he wouldn't miss anything about it except Ruk. Riley hoped he was okay but if the Scouts found out Ruk sabotaged the ship, he would be in terrible danger.

Lulu came charging out of the woods and flopped down at Riley's feet, panting happily and swishing her tail. Her bandage was gone. Riley pulled a flashlight out of his pack and shone it over Lulu's fur, lifting it to check her wound. It wasn't bleeding and the swelling was subsiding.

"I already miss Ruk. We're never going to see him again." Riley tucked the flashlight in his pocket and squatted next to her, running his fingers through her warm fur. It was getting darker and colder by the minute.

Ruk old.

"Probably even older now. We spent eight months on that ship but were only gone from home for an hour. We've been back a whole day; who knows how old Ruk is by now." Riley threw a pebble into the darkness and heard a thud as it hit the ground. An owl hooted and Lulu whuffed an answer.

"I'm kinda glad it wasn't the other way around," Riley said. "It's better that we had to be away all that time instead of Mom and Dad spending eight months thinking we were lost or maybe dead."

Tell Dad.

Riley frowned. "Are you kidding? I can't tell Dad any of this. He'll think I've gone crazy, ranting about spaceships and alternate timelines." He couldn't hold her stare and had to look away. "I'd have to tell him about the fight and that I stole a test from his computer." Riley wasn't sure he could face his dad's disappointment. If he confessed to the theft, he'd have to pay for it as if it had happened just a few days ago – which it had, as far as his dad was concerned. Riley was ashamed of himself but that shame felt old, and he'd had lots of time to think about what he'd done.

Tell Dad.

Lulu poked Riley in the ribs.

"Ow, cut that out!" He tried to shove her away but she pressed against him, whining and licking his hand. Riley scratched Lulu's head, concentrating on the itchy spots while he thought about it. He'd already told Adam and Tina, and they hadn't called him crazy, though he wasn't sure they completely believed him yet.

"Dad already suspects something is going on," he said grudgingly. "He'll notice my left hand soon enough and you won't be able to hide how much you've changed." Riley sighed. "He'll want us both X-rayed and tested, especially you, to prove that you're still you."

No vet. No no no.

"But I know Dad. He'll need convincing evidence. You're supposed to be old and he won't believe you're the same dog unless we can prove you're you. The vet can do tests and show you're the same Lulu."

No vet. Special food.

Riley stared at his dog with new admiration. It was a brilliant idea and he wished he'd thought of it. "It might take most of the special food to bring Dad into our ESP loop. We'll run out way sooner than we expected."

Lulu bark.

"Yeah, I get it. You don't really care if you can hear me in your head."

Lulu licked his face, whining happily. Her whine changed to a growl as she spotted something overhead. She scrambled to her feet, snarling at the sky.

Ship.

Riley stared at the stars until he saw the tiny speck of light that moved slowly across the sky. "Nope, that's a satellite. It's for TV and stuff."

Ship bad.

He put a hand on Lulu's back and felt her tremble. "They won't ever find us again, I promise. Ruk messed with their navigation system and we've smashed the homing beacon."

Riley knew Lulu would eventually forget her fears and the Metarrans would become a dim memory, but until then a distraction might help. "Maybe when Dad knows that I'm almost seventeen he'll finally teach me to drive." He laughed when Lulu's head snapped around to face him, eyes wide.

Car ride?

"Not for a while yet, but yeah, I'll be able to take you for car rides." He stood, brushing dirt from his pants, and fished out his flashlight again. The moon was just coming up but its sliver wouldn't provide enough light to keep from tripping over rocks and roots. He aimed the light into the dark woods, picking out the path that led to the peak of the hill.

"Until then, we do the next best thing." Riley grinned as Lulu sped past him up the path, barking happily.

"We run."

About the Author

Monique Jacob is the author of Tye Dye Voodoo and Voodoo Mystery Tour. She has contributed several short stories to recent Filidh Publishing charity projects, including Anthology for a Green Planet and The UnValentine Anthology.

Monique lives on the West Coast, and can usually be found reading from her recent works at libraries and local cafés. Follow Monique on Facebook and at www.moniquejacob.com.